FOLK OF THE PEAK

RICHARD LITCHFIELD

Published by Country Books
an imprint of
Spiral Publishing Ltd

Country Books, 38 Pulla Hill Drive,
Storrington, West Sussex RH20 3LS

email: jonathan@spiralpublishing.com
www.spiral-books.com

ISBN 978-1-7395303-6-5

British Library Cataloguing in Publication Data.
A catalogue record for this book is available from the British Library.

Printed and bound in England by 4edge Limited,
22 Eldon Way Industrial Estate, Hockley, Essex SS5 4AD

DEDICATION:

To my very own Cyd,
with all a grandfather's love.

SPECIAL THANKS TO:

I would like to express thanks to Sue Rogers, Loreen and Steve Elliott and my wife Caron Robb Jones, for reading my stories and all the encouragement and corrections you suggested. Also to Jonathan and all at Spiral Publishing. You are stars!

SINGING SAM OF DERBYSHIRE

The cover picture is of one man, probably one of the last of his sort, who tramped the Peak District, singing ballads and telling the old folk tales, some of which are reproduced here, and many of which died with Sam and his kind. It was etched in 1760, by which time the 'old ways' were being replaced as the industrial and agricultural revolutions began. There were to be few who came after him

He is described as being dressed in hat and ragged tunic and trousers, and his instrument was a 'rude and single stringed instrument'. It was made from a fully inflated cow's bladder attached to a staff higher than the man himself, and over the bladder was stretched a single string. Sam played this with a bow that consisted of a rough hazel or briar stick, and he passed his hand up and down the string and '...scraped away, and produced sounds which... would no doubt harmonize with Sam's rude ballad and ruder voice.' (Jewitt, Ballads and Songs of Derbyshire, 1867)

We owe a great debt to Sam and his sort, and it is an honour to include his picture in my book.

The picture is courtesy of Derbyshire Record Office. The other illustrations throughout this book are from works by Arthur Rackham (1865 ~ 1937).

Strange to think of those times of old,
And of those who lived there – only a tale,
Doubtingly, dimly, guessed and told...
Look! Listen! The places remain where they lived and died,
To be seen, as they saw them, by you and I:
The scenes of their lives, of their griefs and pride
Telling their tales unmistakably.
The light still shines through the latticed pane
As it shone to them, and the shadowed door
Carries the shade of the shadow they saw.
The rill that runs by the cottage walls
Murmured to them as it murmurs now.
The golden glow of the sunset falls,
As it fell for them, on glade, stream, and bough.
The hall where they feasted, the church where they prayed.
Their cradles, and chambers, and gravestones, stay;
While lord and peasant, youth and maid, rich and poor, have passed away.

But from brittle tome with yellowed page, from mouths long-hushed
We hear, and pass these stories on.
And so we live those lives of old:
And walk with the ghosts of those who've gone.

Freely adapted from a poem by Llewellyn Jewitt
(1816 ~ 1866)

CONTENTS

Introduction	1
The Hob O' the Hearth and the Old Woman	3
Sermon for the Dead	9
Bold Nevison The Highwayman	19
The Tale of the Small-Toothed Dog	27
Hemp Seed I Sow	40
An Irish Maid Would Marry	52
The Pedlar and the Devil	54
Fairy Pipes	70
The Fool and the Feberry Tree	75
A Great Disturbance	82
The Witch and the Young Wife	97
The Butcher and the Devil	104
Smiler and the Hard Stone	114
Crooker	117
The 'Fish-Ghost' of Old Bradwell	124
A Bag of Nuts	131
The Little Red Man, or: The Ginger Feller	135
The Mermaid of the Black Mere	152

INTRODUCTION

I'm not too keen on long introductions, so I will keep my intro short, promise, but what I must tell you is that these stories are, most of them, very, very old, and were collected and first put into print just in time, for they were never written down over the centuries that they were told in, and were dying out when they were collected. They were sought out and published by antiquarians who trawled the Peak District for them in the mid to late 1800's, just before the onset of wireless (radio, that is) early moving films, the record player and then the television.

Every community before the coming of the above attractions had its stories, tales for all occasions, humorous, frightening, sad, and some so weird that they defy explanation. The Peak District was no exception. These stories survived longer because the Peak was, until the railway came, quite a remote place. Defoe famously called it 'an howling wilderness,' and there was one titled fellow (in the seventeen hundreds I believe) who banished his wife to the Peak because he didn't trust her in London. Frankly, I've been to London (oh, yes!) and I know which I prefer. The lady did well out of the deal, I reckon.

A lot of the stories are gone now. Few people sit around a fire with family and friends and tell and swap stories these days, and I have to wonder, with no way of knowing, how many of our folk tales, sadly, have been lost. However, storytelling as an art and as an organised dramatic production has been revived and is thriving, so some of the stories will live a little longer. I remember hosting a storytelling evening once at the wonderful Good For You Café/Restaurant in Matlock some years ago now, and hearing that great storyteller, Graham Langley, tell in his way and words a folk tale I had brought back into print, the wonderful 'the eerie 'Crooker". It gave me a great deal of pleasure to hear it retold, for Crooker to get up and walk again. I was not so pleased a couple of years later to read it in another book that had just been published, as the writer had merely copied large chunks of my story out again, word for word! That was naughty, even if it was a backhanded compliment to my meagre talents, so if you are going to retell these tales, please be inventive, as I hope I have been, and the old storytellers of the Peak were, and tell them in your words, and they will come alive again and float down the years long after you and I are forgotten, and our time is out of mind. I hope you enjoy our stories. As the old storyteller traditionally said, when he or she had finished:

My tale's ended,
T'Door sneck's bended
I went into t'garden to pick a bit o' thyme
I've telled my tale,
Thee tell thine.

THE HOB O'THE HEARTH AND THE OLD WOMAN

Once, time out of mind, there lived an old widow woman, high in the hills of Derbyshire. She lived in a neat and pretty little stone cottage some distance outside of a small village, looking down on the park and gardens of the old squire.

"I want for nothing," she would tell the farmer who called upon her and brought her turves for her fire and straw for her bed. But if the truth be told, she was very, very lonely in her widowhood, for there had been a time when her little cottage was filled with family, when song and laughter had made the dwelling more than just a place to live.

"Still," she would say to herself, "I've food and fire, and there's lots worse off than me!" But inside, something whispered, "Lonely! Lonely!"

One rainy day the farmer called by, bringing her turves and fresh straw, and a basket of food that his wife had prepared for the old lady.

"Eeh! What a bad day, missus," he said, shaking the rain from his shoulders as a dog would. "It's sylin' down! I'm afraid yer straw's a bit damp, an' turves wunner bon in a month er Sundays, an' they say as it's all new squire's fault!"

"New squire?" the old lady asked. "New squire, my lad?

What's happened to the old squire?"

"Anner yer 'eard?" the farmer asked. "Owd Squire 'as died, dahn in London, an' since 'e 'ad no young 'uns 'is nevvy 'as tecken over and cum up 'ere to show us 'ow to do things proper!"

"Oh, no!" said the old woman, her hand to her mouth in shock. "I shall miss the old squire. He was always good to me. Will the new... no, I can't picture a new squire yet. Will the nephew make any changes do you think?"

The farmer snorted. "'E's alreddy made some 'arsh ones! An' now 'e's 'ad ter send fer 'is own London servants 'cos all the owd uns 'ave left." He drew closer to the old woman and said solemnly, "They left 'cos the nevvy's driven out th' hob o' th' hearth, an' nowt'll go right now!"

Now, everyone knew that the old squire had believed in the old ways, in the things that were here long before we were here, and that his luck and long life was because he was fortunate enough to have had living in the hall with him a hob o' the hearth, a spirit which did most of the work by night, and looked after the Squire's interest and his health while he slept. And all the old squire had to do was to leave out a mug of ale and a bowl of good, milky porridge each night. It wasn't known where the squire had come across a hob to befriend, but the squire had been a strange one, right enough. Some of the villagers said that the old squire was one of that rare breed, rare even in those days, half 'fey' himself, and that he could see the hob, and at times spoke to it, but, whatever the case might be, the squire was dead now, and the nephew had drunk the ale left out for the hob, thrown the porridge on the fire, and kicked the servant who had left out the hob's meal for being a waster of good food, and an idle, superstitious fool.

"Mark my words, missus," said the farmer as he took his leave. "If th' hob goes, way'll all suffer. Owd squire should never 'ave gon ter London, nasty, unhealthy place, I say. 'E shoulda' stayed 'ere, wi' 'is own. We'd 'ave looked after 'im!"

It rained all that day, and a cold wind got up. The old woman's fire burned slowly and eventually went out, and she shivered and her bones ached.

"There's nothing for it but to go to bed," she told herself, and wrapping up warm she tried to escape the miserable day by sleeping, but the straw was damp, and there was no fire in the hearth, so she slept badly, hearing each time that she awoke the rain beating against her window and the wind tugging at her door.

In her sleep she thought she heard outside in the driving rain a voice, singing plaintively, lone and lorn:

"When the rain does fall, and the wind do blow,

"What shall I do, and where shall I go?

"Ah, poor me! Ah, poor me!"

Sitting up in bed, the old woman listened again, and heard once more the sad little song. She hobbled to the door and threw it wide on the night, faced into the wind and rain and listened, but could neither hear nor see anything in the coal-black deep beyond her door.

"You're welcome to come in here," she called into the night to whatever poor creature was out there. "I've no fire, and the straw's damp, but I'll leave food on the table, and I dearly would love company, for I am a poor widow woman, all alone in the world, like you, and I will do you no harm."

There came no answer, but as the old woman stepped back from the open door and went to close it, she thought that she saw something small and thin, more like a lithe, brown shadow or a wisp of peat smoke, slip past her skirts and scurry into the furthest corner of her room.

She shook her head and said to herself, "You've been living alone too long, my dear!" and went back to her cold bed, but not before leaving – just in case – a cup of milk and a slice of buttered bread with good Derbyshire sage cheese upon a rough wooden platter.

She awoke the next morning to a changed room. The fire was burning brightly, the dried turves were all stacked neatly by the chimney side, and a pot of something which smelled delicious bubbling contentedly on its hook over the fire. Straw was scattered lightly before the hearth and steamed with a fresh country smell.

And there… yes, there! Something in the darkest corner was sweeping up with a broom, whilst singing in a weird yet gently soothing voice that sounded like a summer breeze across the moor, a curlew calling to its mate, a highland stream bubbling over slabs of mossy limestone. And the song had changed from the night before. Now the hob o' the hearth sang:

"Let the wind blow, let the rain fall,

Hob o' th' hearth has come to your call."

And so the sprite took up his abode with the old woman, and never was the house cleaner and cheerier, for the old woman was happy, properly happy in that quiet, contented way, for all the day long she talked to Hob as she went about her spinning and other tasks, and he would answer from his dark corner near the fire, his voice a sigh, like the wind through the long, tough moorland grass, or chuckle like a grouse in the heather. She was careful not to look directly at him, for hobs are very shy and timid creatures, and soon take fright, aye, and flight! However, if she watched carefully, out of the corner of an eye, she would often see a small, brown, bony figure perched on the turves in a corner, head on knees, staring into the fire as he listened to her, or watching her even, with little, glittering yellow eyes. At night while she slept the hob would clean the house right through and bake oatcakes which the old woman loved to eat, fresh and warm, when she rose.

As spring came the hob would follow the old woman out into her garden while she worked among her plants, and he took up his seat far inside the rocks on the bankside behind her cottage, where a spring flowed out of the hillside. Who knows what he did there, or whether there was another natural spirit living deep inside the rock, a spirit of the water which Hob met with, for the old lady found that the water flowed faster and clearer and tasted sweeter after the hob came to live with her. She drank more of the sweet cold water, and bathed in it often, and she soon found that her aches and pains seemed to be less, and her step was lighter. Some days, she even felt herself to be a maid again and laughed at the thought.

One day the farmer visited her to beg some flowers from her garden.

"Way decoratin' th' well outside our 'ouse," he told her. Missus and eldest lad are getting' rayt dab 'ands at it, an' way mean t' tek prize this year!"

When the farmer had gone, the old woman decided that though she lived outside of the village, she would have her own well dressing, just to please Hob and make his favourite spot beautiful, so she worked all day, digging up and replanting flowers and cutting and arranging other blooms and blossoms around the rocks where the small stream sprang out. Hob must have liked it, for when she left it that night, he worked on, and in the morning she awoke to find her door open, the birds singing in the warm spring sunlight, and beyond, at the bottom of her garden she could see the most beautiful grotto. She ignored the pot bubbling over the fire and the oatcakes still steaming on the hearth – Hob had been busy – and stood in the garden, crying at the beauty of it all.

A sound in the lane made her turn, It was the farmer and his wife and children in a wagon, all in their Sunday best. They had come to take the old woman down to the village to see all the dressed wells and watch the judging of them.

"Well, I'll be…!" gasped the farmer. Yow muster bin as busy as Thrap's wife, doin' that! (And we all know how busy she was, don't we?) Owd on 'ere, ahm off ter fetch th' judges!"

And that year and every year after for as long as the old woman lived (and it was many years, for hobs guard their own very jealously) that old woman had the best-dressed well in the village, and she and the hob lived very happily in their little cottage high in the Derbyshire hills.

You may search the lonely places, on bleak moorland heights where man rarely treads, and the old, crumbling ruins in deserted dales. You may search all over this Peakland for a hob and never find one. They are all lost and gone, lost and gone, and the world is a worse place for it.

SERMON FOR THE DEAD

The new vicar was no stranger to Derbyshire. He had been curate to a parish in the south of the county for several years, but when he came to the Peak, and took over the small and remote parish of Whinfell, he was unprepared for the difference in the countryside with its wild, bleak moors and gritstone outcrops. He had worked amongst a farming community who tilled the soil of lowland, greener pastures, where a silky river flowed gently through, where fat sheep and sleek cattle grazed. Here the river was narrow and fast, bubbling over rocks, brown with peat from the moorland heights. The sheep and cattle were thinner and nimbler, the pastures smaller, with stark, stone walls. The people of this place seemed to be… different to his previous parish. These people seemed freer, more individual and robust, readier to express their opinions, almost a different race. There was something of the pagan about them, he thought, in their enjoyment of life and attachment to their land. Something – he couldn't quite put his finger on it, or put a name to it – spoke of a simpler, older belief that lay behind their faith they professed when they came to his church to worship, as if they were in touch with life and death and the passage of man's life here on earth, and the surety of what lay beyond.

The people of the parish made him welcome, for they had for many years endured the indifference of a non-resident vicar, a distant relative of the aged squire at the Hall, in whose gift the living was. He had left in his absence all church duties to an aged, partially blind curate, and the villagers were won over by the youthful enthusiasm of the new man. They were grateful for his energy and interest on their behalf.

The church became the vicar's pride; it had, by its remoteness, resisted the 'improvements' to the interior of the church that many had been vandalised by. 'His church', as he liked to think of it, had by virtue of its remoteness and the neglect shown by the last incumbent, survived intact, with a three-decker pulpit and a west gallery, which was rarely used, but which had beautiful old carvings to the woodwork and seemed to so perfectly balance the acoustics in the old church that it clearly amplified, and resounded each word of his simple, thoughtful sermons. Once he had thrown out the mouldering rushes on the floor, the rickety benches had been replaced, cracked windows had been reglazed, and the walls freshly white-limed, the church shone with a simple beauty, and the congregation loved the man for giving them back their place of worship.

His first spring was a joy, with preparations for Easter, decorating the church with daffodils from the churchyard, and the choir he had strengthened with new choristers and musicians singing and playing so lustily. On the moors the harebells bloomed so blue on the verges when he was out and about, visiting the sick and elderly and the strange bubbling sound of the curlew enchanted him. Then came preparations for the well dressings, which he entered into heartily, even being honoured by the parish insisting he choose the text and help with the design. He chose the phrase from Isiah 11:6, 'A little child shall lead them' which showed the new world which would be born when Christ came again. He had a hidden reason for choosing the text, for he felt reborn and as if he had entered a heaven on earth.

In the uneventful rounds of parish duties. the young priest passed the first summer and autumn as vicar of Whinfell. And the healthy exercise he took visiting the parishioners in their cottages and distant moorland farms gave new life to him, took away that dry cough and the stabbing pains in the chest that he had endured without mentioning, a little frightened, for the past two years. A solitary man by nature and a sworn bachelor, he suddenly realised how lonely he had been for so long, and he began now to appreciate the unaffected friendship which the Peaklanders offered to him. With a rush of giddy happiness whenever he thought of it, he looked forward to many years serving his parish, belonging here, and never, ever wanting to leave this place which he had come to love so quickly.

So it was that, in the second week of December, when the first disagreement came, he was unprepared for it, and reacted harshly. He had abruptly dismissed the two churchwardens from the unheated vestry where they had come to discuss preparations for the celebration of the Christmas festival with him. The cold and damp weather of late had brought back his chest pains, and the exertion of arguing with the two wardens, one a stolid farmer, the other the village blacksmith, both tremendous support in the past, never opposing him once, made the argument worse, and for a few minutes after they had clumped out of the church in their heavy boots, he stood in a web of pain and sudden fright, hearing his chest give that strange, wheezing sound, feeling the stabs of pain in his lungs. He coughed into his handkerchief, saw the blossom of blood form on the white linen, and felt even more afraid. He had so much to live for now; there was so much still to do.

He stood alone for a while, taking quick and shallow breaths to lessen the pain. He prayed quietly that he would be spared a few more years yet, then sat down on the old iron-bound parish chest to consider the peculiar request the churchwardens had come that night to make of him.

They had come, they said, on behalf of the parish. He being new, and (the farmer had shuffled his feet on the stone floor as he said it) not from these parts, though now one of them and right welcome here… They had tailed off and looked embarrassed until he had prompted them to go on, then they told him that they wished to acquaint him with the tradition of the Sermon for the Dead, which every priest of Whinfell had given on the Sunday after Christmas Day. Not a sermon for those already dead, but a sermon for those parishioners who would die in the coming year, in the belief that the shades of those to die would attend the church that night and would gain comfort from the sermon and guidance for the trial of passing over to another world.

"It's allus bin done 'ere," the farmer said, "and we're 'oping as you'll do it for us."

"We didna think yer'd object," the blacksmith said. "It's a great comfort to us all, and them in the gallery, well, it 'elps them mightily, vicar."

"The gallery?" the vicar asked. "Why, I've never seen a living soul in the gallery all the time that I've been here!"

"Mebbe not," the blacksmith said, looking sheepish but standing his ground. "But they say that the spirits of them that's goin' to die in the parish do creep away from their earthly bodies on that night and gather up in the gallery on the last Sunday of the dyin' year."

The farmer nodded eagerly and added, "They come for to 'ear the words of God, their final judge, vicar, to know that what they 'ave to face can be endured, and that there's a better life waiting for them after all the pain and suffering they've 'ad to endure down 'ere!"

"Such a belief is pagan!" snapped the vicar. "It smacks of witchcraft. I'm sorry, gentlemen, but I'll have no part of it. Why, you'll have me dancing round the Druid's Stones up on Whin Moor next! Now, if you'll excuse me…" and he had shown them out.

In the following weeks he noticed a new reserve, a distance, grow up between himself and his flock, caught them watching him speculatively when he was in the church or out on the village streets, as though they were asking themselves, could we have been wrong about him? Does he care for us, or is he more concerned with his reputation, his standing with the bishop? He ignored this coldness and treated them all the same still. He went about his customary duties, secretly preparing his sermon for the night of the dead, as he began to think of it. What a shock everyone would have! How he would teach them to think differently!

He would, he finally decided, take as his text the passage in First Epistle to the Corinthians which said, 'When I was a child, I spake as a child, I understood as a child, I thought as a child: but when I became a man, I put away childish things.' He would expand on this and show that superstition and blind ignorance were the enemy of a true faith in a living God, that one could not call oneself a Christian and believe in such… such mumbo jumbo!

On the evening of the first Sunday after Christmas, the

last Sunday in a dying year, after they had sung the twenty-third psalm and two hymns, the vicar stepped into the pulpit to give his sermon, and the parishioners went very still, not moving in their seats, a quiet that would have magnified the slightest sound, so that a pin dropped upon the stone floor of the nave would, one imagined, have rung out to the very rafters above.

He opened the great bible on its lectern to the page where he had earlier inserted the silken, tasselled bookmark, nigh as long as his forearm, with his carefully penned outline notes for his sermon lying there too, notes over which he had spent several long nights. He drew a breath, and looked out over his congregation, full knowing that he would hurt their feelings at first, praying that his arguments and close reference to biblical teaching would persuade them to leave the path of pagan superstitions, back into the way of the one true light.

"Dearly beloved brethren… friends… I take for my text tonight…" he began and looked lovingly down upon the villagers below him. In their faces he saw only looks of stubborn resistance, of bewilderment at what they saw as his betrayal of him. Guiltily, he raised his head slightly to avoid their eyes also, and gazed the length of the nave, to the gallery beyond at the back of the building. But what was happening? At the back of the canted gallery, unlit and unused, with the stair door to it locked, he saw in the darkness a sinuous movement, a roiling mist at the back against the stone wall, and lights moved within this mist as it rolled down the steps, over the backs of the pews, towards the front rail. As it rolled it seemed to gain more solidity and become clearer. Bodies were moving inside the mist, he saw with increasing horror, as here a pale hand protruded, bearing a lighted candle, over there the whole form of a body, then another, then more, clad in grave clothes, shrouds and winding sheets, some in white death-hoods, all of them, corpses. Like steam, like mist on a river surface, the white mass rolled forward until it reached the gallery surround at the front, jutting out behind the congregation, and there it bubbled and boiled as the horrified man of the cloth looked upon it, open-mouthed, struck dumb. He fell to his knees, and there was a murmur of concern, the villagers seeing their priest clasping the pulpit edge for support, as if ill. And as he fought to rise, he looked again and saw the mist had gone completely, as if having brought its ghastly company it had retreated to the graves that awaited them all. There standing in a huddle were twenty or so people staring down at him in mute appeal, as real and solid-looking as the congregation below.

The candles they held lit up their faces, and the young priest recognised them all. There was Jem Fisher, old Jem, who had fallen ill last winter, and lay in his low cottage, close to death, but there were others whose live counterparts sat below. Rosy Harris, the publican's wife, who was hale and hearty, a large, healthy woman. Surely not? But there she was, sitting below, and there she also was, in the gallery, staring with a ghastly rictus of death at him, appealing for comfort. And Joe Wilson, Joe, the farmer's son, an ox of a young man, never a day's illness in his life, his parents once proudly told him, who had only last week confided that the vicar would be reading his banns soon, for he planned to marry… He stared down, white-faced at the vicar even as his live body sat like a rock next to his father and mother, with a look of puzzlement on his ruddy face. No, it could not be.

The parson stared from the pulpit to the gallery, then to

the congregation, then back again wildly. How could this be…? And then he saw the ghostly assemblage part, make way for one who stood behind, who came to the fore and looked down at the vicar, eyes burning with the fever that had carried him off, hair plastered to the skull with sweat, the shroud clinging to the emaciated body that had suffered through a short, devouring illness before being wrapped for the grave in its last vestments.

His legs almost gave way as he looked upon this corpse-figure glaring down at him. It was himself! He looked upon the shadow of himself in death! And he had come, as had the others, for a sermon and a blessing, for strength to carry them over the bourne from which none return.

And he had dismissed it as pagan mumbo-jumbo! Even as he thought that he felt the pain in his chest and the lung-wrenching cough came to wrack him again. He wiped the blood from his lips and then raised his head from his chest and stared down upon the congregation. They knew; he could see it in their eyes, yet not one of them dared look behind, up at the gallery, to confirm it. Only he had gazed upon all who would die in Whinfell that year. It was his burden, knowledge that he had to bear as their spiritual guide, and he knew then what he must do. He stepped down out of the pulpit then, and stood before them humbly.

"Friends," he began. "As your vicar of this parish it falls upon me this night to preach the Sermon for the Dead…" There was a gasp from the congregation. He waited for silence, then continued.

"I shall not preach on the intended text but will tell you this one thing as we sit here tonight, with those in the gallery listening too. It is this: no man, woman or child may put their hand to a document which guarantees that they w yeah ill be alive on the morrow. No one can say, here and now to their neighbour, I shall see you tomorrow. No one. This much we know, and so when we think of it, we fear death, and dread what is to come. What shall sustain us? Tonight we sang the twenty-third psalm. Did we reflect upon what the words meant? 'The Lord's my shepherd, I'll not want…' Surely, we shall not! And 'yeah, though I walk in death's dark vale…' brothers and sisters, we all walk in death's dark vale every day, not knowing when our hour cometh. But He knows, and 'yet shall I fear no ill,' for we are told that He is with us, and his rod and staff will comfort us. He will guide us and care for us, and 'in God's house for evermore, our dwelling place shall be.' So what should we fear?"

His sermon was short, but powerful, and as he came to the end, he raised his hands above his shoulders, spreading them wide, and gave a blessing, telling all, both shade and flesh, to go in peace in Christ's name. A great silence came over the building and he raised his eyes and saw that the deathly group was now facing his own shade up in the gallery, which had turned and raised its white, shrouded arms also in blessing. Even as he watched the crowd of spirits turned, his shade kept its arms high and ushered and guided the group back up the steps of the gallery and out through the solid back wall, their candles flicking out as they went.

The congregation left quietly, and the vicar knelt at the altar in prayer for a while, not feeling now the pain in his chest, for he knew that soon he would be bound for a better, an eternal, life.

And when the spring came again to Whinfell, there was a new grave close to the church door, and if a visitor asked whose it might be, for they left it unmarked for a while until the most handsome of headstones could be bought and lovingly inscribed, the villagers would say, "That was our parson. He didn't come from round here, but he was one of us."

(This is an interesting folk custom, and I have never heard of it being observed elsewhere other than in the Peak District, although in the Derby Evening Telegraph of April 13th, 1913 there is mention of a 'Procession of Death' which was believed to happen at nearby Alfreton in Derbyshire. Anybody with nerve enough to sit in the porch of St. Mark's Church on the eve of that saint, which falls on 24th April, his feast day being on the 25th, would see the wraiths of those from the parish who would die in the next year. The paper reports: 'One man, Joseph Dawes, was reputed to have watched and to have been thereafter shunned in case he should disclose the names of those he had seen.' I did read of a man who did this and who sold this information for the rest of the year, though I cannot remember where I read it; it was a long time ago, and, like Grandad's piano, I have lost a lot of my notes over the years.)

BOLD NEVISON THE HIGHWAYMAN

The highwayman is a stock figure in English folklore, and none more famous (or loved, for some strange reason) than Dick Turpin. Most of us know of this famous character's epic ride from London to York in a single day, on his horse, Black Bess. What most people don't know is that the original story about this equestrian record, which is, of course, impossible, is that it was supposed to have been performed by a Pontefract man, John Nevison, a desperado more desperate and dashing than Turpin, and who was supposed to have been kind to the poor, like that other folk hero, Robin Hood. Nevison, also known as 'Swift Nicks', a name given to him along with a royal pardon by Charles II, often ventured into the Peak District on his equally famous horse, Nutmeg, and this story tells of one such occasion.

Cigarette card of John Nevison being presented to King Charles II

Did you ever hear of that hero,
Bold Nevison was his name?
He rode about like a bold hero,
And with that he gained great fame.

He maintained himself like a gentleman,
Besides, he was good to the poor.
He rode about like a bold hero,
And he gained himself favour therefore.

It was market day at Bakewell, and a poor tenant farmer from Padley, who had sold some cattle to help pay his quarterly rent at the coming Michaelmas quarter day, was celebrating his shrewd bargaining with a few strong pints of 'Autumn ale' in the market-room of the Castle Hotel. He drank deeply, but not wisely, and one by one his friends and acquaintances drifted away home as dusk began to fall. At some time during his drinking session a stranger at his elbow fell into conversation with him, a slim young fellow with an easy way about him who bought the farmer drinks and chatted, found out his business and must have seen the farmer's gold pieces when he untied his canvas purse and tipsily insisted on paying his round. After a while when the last of the farmer's friends had left with loud 'Cheer-oh's', the stranger asked for the farmer's advice on the safest way to Sheffield, for, said the stranger, leaning in close, "I carry gold, I can tell you, and don't want some thief on a horse taking it from me!"

All caution lost along with his sobriety, the farmer tapped his nose knowingly, and with a wink told the total stranger that he did too. Then he told him that the best way to Sheffield ran directly past his farmhouse, which was a hostelry as well as a farm, and he unwisely proposed to his newfound friend that they travel as far as Padley together, thinking that the lithe, well-dressed young man who carried himself with such quiet confidence would be added protection. The journey would have to be made in darkness after all, and as he saw the hotel staff lighting lamps along the walls and placing candles on the tables he realised that he didn't relish the ride home on his own. Had he left earlier, he thought, there would have been company enough, for some of the men who had left him drinking at the bar were from the Grindleford area.

Unsteadily, with the young man guiding him by the elbow, the farmer weaved his way over the courtyard to the stables and collected his horse. The stranger had his mount tethered in the yard, a fine-mettled bay, and he swung into the saddle with the practised ease of a good horseman.

"That's a smart steed y'stride," the farmer said, eyeing his new friend's horse admiringly as they trotted out of Bakewell. "And ye ride well, too."

"Aye," the man replied coolly. "It's as best to be well-mounted where the roads are lonely, and robbers abound!"

Little was said on the two-mile pull up to Calver Sough from Hassop, and past there was another stiff climb for the horses up to Tomlin Gate. At the summit they paused to 'breathe' their mounts, mainly for the farmer's tired old sway-backed nag, then they rode slowly down the road towards Stoke Hall. Under the dark beech trees a ghostly white barn owl swooped over the two men's heads, and the stranger's horse was unsettled slightly, skittering sideways a short distance.

"Steady, Meg!" the stranger said, patting its neck and talking soothingly as one would to a child. "Steady my sweet Nut!"

"Meg? Nut? Nutmeg!" the farmer gasped. His head had cleared in the crisp autumn air since they had left Bakewell. "Why, Nutmeg's the mount of..."

"John Nevison at your service, sir!" said Nevison, producing a long pistol, "And I'll thankee for your purse, my good man."

"Don't take my money," the poor farmer pleaded. "I sold some of my cows to pay the rent at Michaelmas. There's a murrain on the cattle in Yorkshire and no beasts are being allowed in from the North, so I got a good price, but if this goes it will break me."

Nevison pressed the muzzle of his horse pistol into the farmer's chest and held out his other hand for the farmer's purse.

"If you take this, I am finished. It's all the money I have in the world, and if I don't pay my rent I'll be thrown off my farm. I have a wife and children, and we'll be paupers if I lose this gold."

Nevison clicked back the hammer of his pistol and pressed the muzzle even more firmly into the man's chest. Nutmeg snorted and pawed the ground, as if eager to be galloping away into the night. From a distance an owl hooted. With a heavy heart the farmer reached inside his shabby old greatcoat and brought out the canvas purse which contained his gold.

"Well," said Nevison as he pocketed the gold, "As it's your rent money, and you're a poor man, it shall be repaid. I do not rob the poor. But I have need of this money now, and it wants ten days till Michaelmas, by my reckoning. Before then I shall visit you and return your money, my good sir. You have my word upon it. Hi, Nutmeg! Away!"

With that, Nutmeg sprang forward into the night, and before the farmer could collect his befuddled wits, the hoofbeats of Nevison's fine horse could be heard drumming away into the distance.

Nine worrying days passed for the farmer, who had but two main thoughts all that time: Will Nevison keep his promise? What shall I do if he doesn't? The lord who owned the farmer's land was a cruel master and showed his tenants no mercy or leeway in the matter of debts that were called in, such as rent. Not a day's grace, thought the wretched tenant, and as the days wore on he kept thinking to himself, five days and we are paupers, four days and we are on the road, three days and…

On the ninth day, with rent due on the morrow and no sign of Nevison, the farmer sat up until midnight in the parlour of his hostelry, long after the last customer had gone. Finally he barred the doors, lit a candle and made his way up the stairs to where his unsuspecting wife lay, softly breathing into a goose-down pillow. Ah, the simple pleasures of life, the farmer thought, looking down on her lovely face. A roof over one's head and a bed to lie in after the day's hard work. Where would she lay her head tomorrow? Soon they would have neither hearth nor home.

He donned his nightgown and sat glumly on the bed. Suddenly there came the sound of a shot from the direction of Grindleford Bridge, a loud report like that of a musket or rifle, then a sharper 'crack!' of a pistol in reply. In those days there was a sentry box , upon the bridge, and the local men took it in turns to guard this entry to the village through the dark hours of the night. There were extra men watching out for anyone trying to get cattle past the bridge and into Derbyshire, because there was a 'murrain', a disease among the northern cattle, and drovers from Yorkshire had been bidden to stay away for fear of spreading the disease further south.

The night was still and clear, and the sound of gunfire

echoed along the valley, from Frogatt to Sir William, over the ridges of Cicely Tor and Tedgness. As the farmer listened he heard a horse, galloping wildly up from the bridge towards his hostelry, and upon reaching his house, it was reined in by a shouted command

"Hold, Nut! Hold, my gal!"

There came a smash from below, as the windowpanes shattered under impact from a heavy object, and the noise awakened the children who began to cry from their bedrooms. The farmer's wife awoke blearily, her nightcap falling over one eye and calling out in fear. Over the hullabaloo could be heard the night-rider's hooves as he headed off into Padley Woods, safe from all pursuit, should any care to risk their life in following such an able and determined horseman.

It was Nevison who had called. He had called in at a hostelry on his way to Grindleford, but this time he had been 'rumbled'. Someone had recognised Swift Nicks, and he had been chased by a party of young bloods eager to claim the reward that was on his head. He had outrun his pursuers, and had forded the river below Grindleford Bridge, knowing about the night watch that was stationed there. A keen-eyed guard had seen him, taken a pot-shot, and Nevison had returned fire, and perhaps because Nevison's reply had been too accurate, for the highwayman was supposed to be a crackshot with a pistol, the guard prudently decided that honour had been satisfied, and did not attempt to give chase. For many years after, the musket which had fired upon the infamous highwayman was displayed on the wall of a local inn.

When the farmer and his family reached the room below, Nevison was long gone, but a child bent over and picked up from among the broken glass and pieces of splintered window frame a canvas bag. He handed it to his father. Inside was the money which had been taken from the farmer ten days before, plus an extra golden guinea, wrapped in a scrap of paper, on which was written, 'Interest for the loan of rent money, with thanks.'

Bold Nevison, Gentleman of the Road, had kept his word.

Sadly, but predictably, Nevison met the end of most highwaymen. Despite receiving a royal pardon for past crimes, he continued his chosen way of life, and as his notoriety and the reward for his capture both increased he became a target for bounty hunters and common 'snitches', as well as the law. After killing one such 'thief taker' called Fletcher, Nevison was recognised taking refreshment at an inn, arrested and tried, and after a bewigged judge told him that 'he must dye, for he was a terrour to the country,' Swift Nicks 'danced on air' as the criminals of the day termed hanging, at Knavesmire, Yorkshire, on 4th May 1684.

'Tis now before the Lord Judge,
Oh, guilty or not do you plead?
He smiled unto the judge and jury,
And these were the words that he said:

It's when I rode upon the highway,
I've always had money in store,
And whatever I took from the rich,
I freely gave to the poor.

I have never robbed no man of tuppence
And I've never done murder nor killed.
Though guilty I've been all my lifetime,
So gentlemen do as you please.

THE TALE OF THE SMALL-TOOTHED DOG

Once upon a time, long, long ago, only a few years after Adam were a lad, there lived in the Peak District a merchant prince who was very, very rich. Now, a merchant prince is not a real prince. Oh, no, my lovelies. A merchant prince is a trader who has a lot of valuable goods and a big heap of money he keeps somewhere safe. This merchant prince dealt in lead from the Derbyshire hills and salt from Cheshire, Staffordshire wool, Nottingham lace, and gold and silver, and cloth and food and, well, anything that could turn a bob or two, as they say. He travelled frequently to trade with other merchants and had brought back from far countries many strange items, which were very valuable too. But the dearest thing to his heart, which he prized above all else was his daughter, who, as in all good stories, was passing fair, which means incredibly beautiful.

One day the merchant saddled his favourite horse, which he called Ker-Ching! because that was, next to his daughter singing in her bath, the most beautiful sound in all his world, and that sound was the pretty tune an old-fashioned cash till makes when it's opened: Ker-Ching! goes the little bell, and, thank you, sir or madam, a little richer grows the merchant. Now, Ker-Ching! came from a distant land and was a talking horse with a taste for literature. Of course, neither the horse or the merchant let other people know that Ker-Ching! could talk or he might have been stolen. Cunningly, the merchant often left his horse standing near other traders while he was out of earshot, and Ker-Ching! listened and passed onto the merchant the traders' plans and the true prices they would charge or buy for goods that his master either had or wanted. I'll tell you, there were no flies on either the merchant or his horse. House flies, or horse flies, that is.

Throwing his saddlebags over the horse's back, the merchant mounted, waved goodbye to his daughter where she sat in the window of his very posh house and set off.

"Where to, Chief?" asked Ker-Ching! the horse.

"Take me in search of gold and silk under foreign skies," commanded the merchant, thinking to himself, got him this time.

The horse ruminated a while as he trotted along then said, "That's a bit of Flaubert, the great French writer, unless I'm much mistaken."

Drat, thought the merchant, then said slyly, "I loved his 'Count of Monte Cristo'."

"Come on, Boss," the learned steed snorted. That's Alexandre Dumas, and well you know it!"

"Can't fool you," said the merchant.

"Flaubert also said, and it's apposite to the hour, methinks," Ker-Ching! mused, "'Travel makes one modest. You see what a tiny place you occupy in the world.'"

"Now you're just showing off," said the merchant, shaking the reins. "Enough! Take me to strange and foreign lands whose tongues I do not speak."

"Wirksworth it is," said the horse, and turned his head

southward. After a while, as they drew near to dear old Wussa, the horse said, "Daniel Defoe visited these parts y'know. Called it 'An howling wilderness'."

"I know," said the merchant. "Defoe, Treasure Island."

"Robinson Crusoe," the horse snapped. "Treasure Island is Stevenson. Credit me with some intelligence!"

And so the jolly badinage went on, filling both horse and rider with much entertainment to while away the hours, for in truth, they were the best of friends and enjoyed each other's company. Reaching Cromford the merchant referred to it as a place of 'Rough quarries, rocks and hills whose heads touch heaven,' and Ker-Ching! was quiet until they had passed the old Bell Inn, before he said, "Willy Wobbledagger, Othello, the tragic Moor, speaking," but as the merchant had dismounted to spare his horse, and was finding the hill hard going, he was too out of puff to retort.

They passed out of the Peak, journeyed through Derbyshire and found themselves in lands that were indeed strange, where, on the maps of the day it was sufficient to mark, 'Here there bee dragonnes,' as a fancier way of saying, 'You are on your own, old son.'

"This," said the horse, pulling up in the middle of a dense wood and looking around him, "looks like the sort of place inhabited by:

...the cannibals that each other eat,
The Anthropophagi, and men whose heads
Do grow beneath their shoulders."

"Spokeshave the immortal bard, and Othello again," the merchant said, absent-mindedly, for he was wondering to himself what that rustling noise was in the undergrowth, and why he suddenly felt as if he and Ker-Ching! were being watched.

They were indeed being surveyed, evaluated, and discussed with no friendly intent, by three of the worst villains in the area, their names being Smacke, Grabbitte, and Scarper, desperadoes known to the rather inadequate forces of law and order in those parts as footpads of the worst kind.

A footpad, not to be confused with a brake pad, was really a highwayman who was saving up to buy a horse, a low thief who threw violence in as an optional extra, optional on their part, that is. Since footpads didn't, by definition, own horses, they were easily caught, and theirs was usually a short-lived career. Most of them went legit when the car was invented.

Smacke, Grabbitte and Scarper lived in a lair above the woods, and of them and their forays it was written by that well known author, poet and graffiti artist, A. Non:

'Forth from their lair to steal they stole,
Their bags of chink they chunk,
And many a wicked smile they smole,
And many a wink they wunk.'

"I say," said Ker-Ching!, "there's a bunch of ruffians surveying us from beyond yonder bush. Now might be a good time to draw and brandish that good sharp sword you always..."

"Drat" said the merchant, snapping his fingers, "I knew there was something I'd forgotten when we set out! Howsomever, my courage always rises at every attempt to intimidate me."

"Jane Austen," murmured the horse, wheeling to face the ruffians.

Forth from the concealing foliage sprang the three footpads, smiling smoles of malice, and winking wunks to each other.

"Stand and deliver!" roared Smacke. "Seize them, men!"

"Yes, grab them, my underlings!" shouted Grabbitte, who also wanted to be top man. "Throw down your chink so that we may chunk it!"

"Yes, bosses!" shouted Scarper, who was a little lacking in self-confidence and only hung around with the other two to boost his image. He leaped forward and pulled the merchant from his horse. The merchant, who was somewhat portly from good-living, fell heavily, and the three rascals laid about him with a will and their cudgels which I forgot to mention.

"Unhand me villain!" shouted the wealthy trader to one footpad, and Ker-Ching! murmured, "Title of short story by Robert Erin Howard, inventor of Conan the Barbarian. Really, this is getting ridiculous…"

Whackety whack! The footpads went, and ouchy ouchy! went the poor merchant as Grabbitte and Smacke gave him what for, while Scarper grabbed Ker-Ching!'s bridle and tried to see what was in the saddlebags.

"I give in!" cried the merchant, rolling on the floor.

"Not till we've finished!" snapped Smacke. "We like to do a thorough job."

Just as all seemed terribly bleak for the merchant and his poor horse, into the clearing bounded the largest dog anyone had ever seen. Talk about Newfoundlands? Psshah, I say, mere infants!

"Stroll on!" gasped Ker-Ching! managing in the confusion to get a good nip in on Scarper's botty. "You don't see many of those at Cruft's!"

With a woof and a deep growl, the dog set about the three footpads, knocked them all down in the dust of the road, gave them a jolly good scufting and routed them, inflicting upon Scarper another nip to the botty as he scarpered, but on the other cheek for the sake of symmetry. They ran and ran till they reached their lair and dived into its depths. So bad a fright did these baddies get that they foreswore any more footpadding and took to legitimate work, becoming traffic wardens, and thus could continue robbing honest travellers.

The merchant was in a bad way, and the huge dog sniffed him all over and then said to Ker-Ching!, "He's in a bad way." He gently placed the poor unconscious merchant onto his broad doggy back, and barked out to the horse, "Gallop after me!" and set off for his home, Ker-Ching! complaining that he was in pain too. The dog made some sort of terrible joke about a 'stable condition' then ignored the poor equine, who hobbled on behind him.

The huge canine led the complaining Ker-Ching! to a remote but beautiful mansion where he bathed and bandaged the merchant's wounds. He also treated Ker-Ching! for a chipped hoof and extracted some footpad's trouser-bottom from between his teeth.

The merchant slowly recovered after many weeks of careful nursing, and once he was fit to travel home again, he went in search of the dog, who was stretched out on his patio with a large bone, chewing casually as he watched Ker-Ching! crop his front lawn.

"I say, Doggie, old chap," the merchant said awkwardly, "I am terrifically grateful to you. You saved my life, and I would like to repay you with whatever you wish that I possess. Name it and it shall be thine."

The huge dog waved a massive front paw nonchalantly, and said, "Think nothing of it. A dog is a man's best friend, after all. That's A. Non, by the way."

"But I *must* reward you," the merchant said, and he dived

in his huge saddlebags and produced a small, blue fish in a jar.

"Will you take my fish from far Zanzibar, which can speak twelve languages?" he asked.

The dog chewed his bone thoughtfully and regarded the fish.

"Can't stand pet fish," he said. "The way they open their mouths y'know? Always look as if they are screaming underwater. Anyway, twelve languages? I only speak one language… I *do* know a little Alsatian, however. He's called Rex. Lives down the road from my aunty. Joke, that. Sorry."

The merchant rummaged deeper in his saddlebags and eventually came up with a somewhat indignant and ruffled-looking goose.

"Hate to let it go," the merchant said, "but what about a goose that lays golden eggs? Got this fine specimen in far Cathay. Twenty-four carat gold eggs!"

"Make such a mess of your lawn," the dog said. "Nasty, smelly things, geese. Went to Kedleston Hall once. The mess those geese had made of the area round the lake! Yuk!"

"Got it!" said the merchant, digging deeper. "From the fabled gasworks – sorry, I mean glassworks – of Venice. A mirror that shows you what others are thinking!"

The dog cracked open the bone and sucked thoughtfully at the marrow within.

"Can't hold a mirror with paws," he said, apologetically. "Anyway, people tend not to try and deceive me. Always goes badly for them if they do."

"So, what can I give you of great worth to show my gratitude? Name it! Anything!"

"Anything?" asked the dog. "Quite literally, anything?"

The merchant nodded and crossed his heart.

"There is one thing which you possess," said the dog

slowly, spitting out a splinter of bone from between his small teeth, "and that is your beautiful daughter, the fairest in the land. I would like her to come and live in my beautiful mansion so that I can see and hear her every day and look upon her beauty."

I know, the cheek of it, eh? But things were very different in those days, and some fairy tales tend to be very, very sexist. And the fact remains that in days of old, when dogs were bold, et cetera, that a daughter was regarded as the property of the father. Not of the mother, as the husband owned her as well. Terrible state of affairs. But, as a writer once said, the past is a foreign country, they do things differently there. Can't remember who said it...

"L.P. Hartley, in his famous novel, The Go-Between," said Ker-Ching!, peering over my shoulder, then, to the merchant he whispered, "I say, Merchie, have you noticed that dog's teeth? They're very small!"

But the merchant wasn't listening. He knew the dog had him bang to rights. After all, he was a man of commerce, and a man was only as good as his word. If it ever got around that he had refused to honour a deal, he was done for. So, reluctantly, he agreed, and the dog chased his tail in delight for a while, then said that in a week he would show up at the merchant's house and collect said daughter, giving the trader time to prepare his daughter to the idea of being swapped so casually.

"Sooner you than me," said Ker-Ching! "She's very nice, but boy! does she have a temper!"

Brooding upon this, the merchant and his horse headed home and great was the daughter's joy at seeing Daddy home again. Ker-Ching! sloped off to his stable somewhat hurriedly, but later, once the merchant broached the subject of the deal Ker-Ching! still heard every word through the limestone walls, even though he buried his head deep in the hayfeeder. Eventually he heard the beautiful young woman say to her father that, very well, she would go, but she intended to make her father's life a misery for the next week, and the dog's life even worse until he released her from the vow that bound her.

Sure enough, after a week the giant, small-toothed dog came galloping through the Peak right up to the door of the merchant's mansion.

"Stroll on!" gasped the daughter, "You don't see many of those at…"

"It's been done," said Ker-Ching! gloomily. "Gonna miss you, kid."

"I'll be back," she promised, as the dog picked her up and galloped off, faster than the wind, with his prize on his back.

Arriving at the dog's beautiful mansion, the girl dusted herself down, complained loudly of having got fleas from 'the filthy mutt', and insisted on giving him a very thorough bath in very smelly disinfectant. That done, she strolled into the house and slipped itching powder into his golden dog basket. The dog spent a most uncomfortable night, itching with the powder and sneezing at the disinfectant smell. The merchant's daughter, on the other hand, or paw, spent a quite refreshing night, having commandeered the best bedroom and the softest bed, and putting the dog's basket in the draughty hallway, to add to his discomfort.

After a month of making the dog's life a trial (not a sheepdog trial, just a plain, generic one), the young tyrant demanded that the dog take her back to visit her father.

"All right," said the dog, weakened by all the torments inflicted. Anything for a bit of peace, "Just for three days. A long weekend. But first, what do you call me?"

"You are a great, foul small-toothed dog," she snapped, stamping one dainty, soft-shod foot on the floor, and that was a biiiiiiig mistake, oh yes!

"Then you shall not go," said the dog and padded off to scrounge a bone from the cook.

Oh, great was the maiden's chagrin, and she changed into her big clumpy goth boots and stamped and wailed so much that the dog came back.

"What do you call me now?" he asked, only weakening because the domestics were threatening to hand in their notices and the cook did the nicest roasted marrow bones he'd ever chomped on.

"Oh, your name is 'Sweet-as-a-honeycomb'," she said sickeningly, and even managed a dimple for the poor sap.

"Jump up, sweetykins," said the mammoth mutt, lifting one hairy leg to the horizontal as a step, a little like elephants do, and off they galloped towards her home.

They raced over hill and dale for several leagues, because miles hadn't been invented yet (and as for kilometres, don't get me started), until they were near the merchant's gaff, and the dog put his rider down and asked her again:

"What do you call me?"

Scornfully the girl replied, "You are still a great, foul, small-toothed dog!"

That did it! The dog leaned forward, grabbed her by the back of her hoody in his small teeth and flipped her up into the air like a Winster Shrovetide pancake. As she tumbled down, he walked underneath, caught her on his massive back and away they went, back to the Dog House. Takes a while with some people, doesn't it?

Right, thought the merchant's daughter when she got

back to the dog's mansion, time to step up the annoyance factor a mite. And she locked herself in her room and played, at full volume, a CD she had in her collection: The Pensioners of Matlock Massed Kazoo Band Play Status Quo (they lost, five-nil). On the second day the cook handed in her resignation, and on the third the deaf butler and the rest of the household staff did likewise.

"That's it!" yelled the dog. "Enough!"

"Oh, don't you like it?" the merchant's daughter asked innocently. "I've got them doing Acid Rock, as well. With Ezra Toft conducting. Flawless production on that album…"

"Get your gear. I'm taking you home," the peerless pooch proclaimed.

"Yes!" chortled the girl, and she leapt upon the dog's back.

Halfway there the dog stopped.

"What do you call me?" he asked, and the girl stroked his head lovingly, and cunningly told him that he was 'Sweet-as-a-honeycomb'. The dog lolled a great pink tongue out happily, for the truth was that annoying as she had been, he had fallen quite badly for her.

They came to the merchant's palatial home, and the girl slid down the dog's hairy flank and ran to the door. With her hand on the latch, she heard the dog ask softly, "Before you go, what do you call me now?"

She turned, her eyes flashing with temper, and was about to say something really nasty and cutting, like "You are a great foul, smelly, flea-ridden…" when she saw a tear well up in each of the dog's large, sad, brown eyes, and she remembered then how he had saved her father's life, how he had nursed the old merchant back to health, how gentle and loving and good-tempered he had been while she had lived at his house. Now he was crying at their parting! Suddenly she realised that she loved the great big bowser!

She threw her arms as far around the colossal neck as she could manage and wept into his fur, "You are not, you are my Sweetikins, my sweeter-than-a-honeycombe doggykins and I love you vewwy vewwy much!" Ewwww! And she planted a few wet kisses on his bulbous, 'normous black nose.

At the words "I love you," an amazing thing happened! The giant dog reared up on his hind legs and his fur split all the way down his tummy, and his head tilted back like the lid of a bean tin, and out of the dogskin stepped a handsome young man, with golden hair and deep blue eyes and a complexion like peaches and cream. He stepped forward and, taking the maiden's hands, he kissed her fingers gratefully.

"What...? Who...? When...? Why...?" the maiden gasped, totally amazed.

The young man, formerly known as 'Dog' looked a mite embarrassed. He shuffled his paws, I mean... feet.

"I er... ran into a... er... wicked witch," he said.

"Oh, yes?" the girl said, sniffing, "Let me guess, old, was she? Poor? Ragged clothes? Bit bent over? Wart in the nasal area?"

"That's the old crone!" The ex-dog shouted excitedly. "Do you know her? No? Oh, well, if you do run into her..."

Mmmm..., thought the girl. Patronising, patriarchal outlook, sexist, chauvinist stereotyper. Going to have to put this one straight if I decide he's a keeper... Captivate, Isolate, Educate, girl.

"So?" Prompted the girl, "What happened?"

"Well, said the young man, "I told her she was an old fraud, and the last thing I remember is her saying she'd cast a spell that would stop me laughing. And I laughed again, and said, er… Go for it, basically."

"And…?"

"And she pointed a finger at me and said, 'Dog thou art, and dog shall be, till the purest love shall set you free,' and there was a sort of boom of thunder and a cracking like lightning, and I fell over, and 'hello, Fur City!' But you set me free, with your pure love for me and…"

"Pure love for a dog," the maiden corrected. "Don't get any fancy ideas."

Stepping forward the handsome young hunk took the maiden's hands and kissed her fingers, while staring into her beautiful green eyes.

"I love you," he sighed. "I have loved you since I first beheld you. Please say you will be mine!"

Strewth! he's tall, she thought, looking up at him. Must be six-three if he's a day. And he's buff, too. Not like most of the lads round here, they're all dogs. Oops!

"Oh please!" he begged. "Marry me, oh moon of my delight that knows no wane!"

"Edward Fitzgerald!" shouted Ker-Ching! from a nearby meadow.

"From the Rubaiyat of Omar Khayyam, first edition, published 1859, nailed it!" shouted the wealthy merchant from the open window of his counting house. "Bring the lad in, duck!"

"I think a bath first, Dad!" she shouted back. "He's been inside a dog skin for absolutely yonks without bathing. He don't half niff!"

"You mean… you will… we will… we'll live happily after?" the young man gasped.

"We'll see," the merchants daughter said, taking his hand in hers. "Come on, bath first, followed by some new clobber from our stock, then we'll go and meet Dad. And one more thing..."

"Yes?"

"Stay off the furniture!"

HEMP SEED I SOW

Now, this story didn't happen yesterday, nor even the day before, but a very, very long time ago. This was a different time, when people lived simpler, harder lives, when they were more in touch with their surroundings, and they believed many different things that we would scoff at as silly superstitions nowadays. But maybe the fact that our ancestors were more open to the world around them and believed such things *could* happen made them truer, even *caused* them to happen… Who is to say? Anyway, here is the story…

In a dale outside of Ashbourne there lived a young farmer and his wife Mary, and a very happy life they lived together. They worked hard, he with his flock of sheep and small herd of dairy cattle and crops of barley and hay, and she in the dairy, a-milking and making of cheese and butter which they sold on Ashbourne market. Together they lived and together they thrived.

Mary was a beautiful woman, strikingly so, with a mass of dark, flowing hair, and eyes as dark black as obsidian, teeth that flashed white against deep-coral lips when she smiled, and a voice so sweet she could have charmed the birds from the branches if she so wished. Some in the town of Ashbourne below the dale said she was of foreign blood, a throwback from a drover who came down from the highlands of Scotland and stayed for some reason, others said she was of Spanish gypsy blood, for didn't her family on the father's side send sons for several generations into the Kings' armies and fight abroad in their service? Perhaps one brave soldier boy had brought a foreign sweetheart home, and Mary was the living witness to it. There were a few who said she had special 'gifts', and she would have 'hunches' that came true; she could tell fortunes by looking at a person's hand, or just holding it. And sometimes, for special friends, she would 'read the cards' or look into a pool of ink and 'scry'. Some there were in the town who did not approve of such practices, and they said that only a few years ago she would have been in trouble with the Church authorities, could even have been hanged for a witch, but Mary would give one of her very peculiar little chuckles and say, "It's always been around, and it always will be."

Mary and John had been married for ten years, and dearly longed to have a child, but Mary miscarried twice, and both a physician and a midwife in the town told the couple that if she became with child again and wanted to keep it then she must do no work and take to her bed. Even so, it would be dangerous for Mary to try for more children, they said, but when Mary was thirty-two, she told John that she was expecting again. This child, she told John, would – with care – live.

Mindful of the doctor's warning, John said that he would hire help to do Mary's work, and she would rest until their child was born. A young woman from Ashbourne was employed to do Mary's work in the dairy, and John told her he would hire a maid from the town to do the housework and look after her during the day while he was working the farm, so he let it be known he was hiring, and several young women came up to the farm the following day and knocked on the door.

Mary watched from her window upstairs, where she lay in bed. She called John up and said to him, "John, we want the right type of girl. Just go down and place my broom across the path, by the doorstep, there's a duck." John went as if to question her, and she added, "Humour me, love. You shall see."

A puzzled John did as she said and placed the broom right across the last flagstone in front of the door. The first girl arrived to be questioned as to her experience and stepped right over the broom to knock on the door.

"No, John," said Mary. "She won't do. Send her away – and... John? Leave the broom where it is if you please."

The next girl walked up the path, stopped at the broom, picked it up and leant it against the wall by the door.

"Hmmmm...," said Mary. "Not quite there yet, I'm afraid. Send her away, please John. She won't suit."

The last girl, a young woman with bright red hair and an open, ruddy face, bustled up the path, shooed the hens out into the farmyard, closed the gate, then picked up the broom, swept the path and the doorstep, and leant the broom against the wall, dusting her hands together and looking to see if she'd missed any dirt or a stray feather before she knocked on the door of the farmhouse.

"She's the one!" said Mary with her strange little chuckle. "Send her up, John. I rather think she'll do!"

The young woman's name was Alice Webster. She came into the bedroom, bobbed to 'Mum' as she chose to call Mary, and immediately began rearranging the bed Mary was in, plumping up the pillows and straightening the quilt over the invalid. Within the hour, Mary had had a wash from Alice and was sitting with a cup of beef tea while Alice prepared 'the Master's' evening meal, a hearty beef casserole with boiled potatoes and greens from the garden.

Alice proved to be a treasure, both hardworking and a companion to Mary as she lay for long days in her bed or nestled in a chair by the farmhouse range. The young girl was an accomplished cook, could sew, keep a kitchen and household as well as any older woman, and was very attractive – and single! Mary was surprised that Alice was not married, and didn't even seem to have a young man. She was such a catch for any sturdy Ashbourne fellow who had his head on right, she thought often.

That subject came up one night as Alice helped Mary prepare for bed. Christmas had passed, and the new year, and St. Valentine's Day was coming up. It so happened that the saint's day fell on a Sunday, and Alice came and asked if she could go home on Saturday afternoon to see her sister, who had just had a baby. She would stay the night with her widowed mother, who lived in a cottage by the church in Ashbourne and come back on Sunday morning, she promised.

"I know why you're really going home," Mary teased. "You want to be at home on Valentine's Day, when the flowers and the notes pile up at your door!"

(This was in the days before Valentine's cards were invented, and a swain in love would show his affections with flowers, notes, even love poems, left at the door of the woman he loved (no postmen, either!).

Alice laughed and said, "Oh, Mum, no one wants an old maid like me! I'm nearly twenty, and never been kissed!"

"Nonsense!" Mary said. "You would be a catch for any

young Ashbourne lad who came a-courting!"

There was quiet for a while, as Alice helped Mary into bed and arranged the bedclothes over her, fastened a bedjacket and sleeping cap over Mary's head, her long black tresses shining against the white linen. It was then that Mary said slyly, "Would you like to know if you will marry, and who he will be?"

"Ooh, Mum," said Alice excitedly, "I've been told you can…"

Mary arched an eyebrow at the young servant.

"I can… what?" she asked softly.

"Oh, Mum! You know full well what I mean," Alice laughed. "You have the sight, the gift, whatever you want to call it."

Mary gave her little chuckle, and Alice shivered with excitement.

"I know one way to tell," the good wife said.

"I've tried putting my shoes under my bed," Alice said, "You know, right below my head, in a T shape, then I said the spell three times: 'I've put my shoes in the shape of a T, hoping my true love to see. Let him be young, let him be old, let him come and visit me.'"

"And?" Mary asked.

"Didn't work! You're supposed to dream of your husband to be, but I didn't dream at all," Alice said scornfully.

"I know one way, an old charm," Mary said, settling into her pillows and pulling the bedcurtains right up to the wall by her head, so Alice had to peer round them. It was a cold night.

"Oh, tell me, Mum, please!" Alice begged.

"Well," said Mary, "Go to the barn and find the hemp seed in two big sacks there, over at the back. Take a double handful – use one of the linen bags in that chest at the end of the bed. Now, you must follow this carefully for it to work…"

"Oh, I will! I will!" Alice said, excitedly, "Does it really work, Mum?"

Mary nodded, slowly, her dark eyes on the maid's face.

"Take your hemp seed, and on St. Valentine's Eve, go you to Ashbourne churchyard as it's about to strike midnight. At the first note of the bell, run round the church twelve times widdershins (anti-clockwise, the witch's direction, as it was known, against the course of the sun), scattering the hemp seed with your left hand, and repeat, without stopping, this rhyme:

I sow hempseed, hempseed I sow,
The man that I'll marry
Come, and after me mow."

"And will it work?" Alice asked eagerly. "Do you know of any as have tried it, Mum?"

"Never fails," said Mary. "I know two women who have tried it…"

"Who were they?"

Mary looked steadily and solemnly at Alice.

"Elsie Cook and Gladys Hill," she said.

"But… they aren't married, never have been! They're old maids!" said Alice.

"Exactly," said Mary, and gave her low chuckle, "They went round twelve times and saw – nothing, nobody!"

"Oh, Mum!" Alice screamed, laughing till she bent over and had to sit at the end of the bed, wiping her eyes. "You fair caught me there. Just the same…"

"Just the same, what, Alice?"

"I'm going to give it a go," Alice said, and fetched a linen bag from her mistress's linen chest to hold the hemp seed.

The next afternoon, Alice left late as the sun set, and as she stepped out of the door of Mary's bedroom, she gave her mistress a broad wink, and patted her apron pocket, which bulged with the bag of hemp seed she had filled in the barn when John was not watching.

"That girl!" sighed Mary, and gave her usual low chuckle.

Sunday morning, quite early, John got up and began his labours around the farm before setting off for church. He'd only been gone for five minutes when Mary heard the latch on the door downstairs lift, and young Alice came running up the stairs and burst through the door, throwing off her coat and bonnet.

"Oh, Mum!" she gasped, and sat down with a bump on the bottom of the bed.

"Good morning, dear," said Mary, "What ails you? You look so flushed!" Then she saw that Alice was laughing, indeed laughing so hard that her face was red, and that her freckles had all but disappeared under the blush.

"Ooh, Mum!" Alice said, "Last night…"

"You went?" Mary asked. "Really? You went to the church at midnight? I thought you wouldn't go through with it, all alone at midnight in a graveyard."

"Huh!" said Alice. "My old dad used to say it's not the b******s below ground you need to fear, it's the b's still walking around that you need to watch out for!"

"So, what happened?" Mary asked. "Did the charm work?"

Alice tossed her head.

"No!" she laughed. "Of course not, silly idea, really. But I didn't get chance to run round twelve times, mind you…" She stopped and looked keenly at her mistress.

“You didn’t put Master up to it, did you?” she asked suspiciously.

“Master? John? No, of course not,” Mary answered. “Oh, Alice, I swear, if you don’t tell me what happened soon, I shall leap out of this bed, baby and all, and box your ears for you!”

Alice hutched herself along the bed and leant over conspiratorially.

“Well,” she said, “I’d no sooner got up to the church porch and got my hemp seed out and taken a handful, than the church bell struck the first note of midnight. So, off I goes, running round and chanting, ‘I sow hempseed, hempseed I sow…’ You know, Mum…”

“Yes?” Mary asked, leaning forward so that their heads nearly touched. “Come on, tell me!”

Alice began to laugh again and had to put her hand to her mouth and get her composure back again.

“I only got the verse out once and I saw someone come in from the town end, through the gate, and walk up the path, all hunched over, like and wavering a bit, as if he had been drinking, and I looked and who was coming towards me but…” she started to laugh again, and Mary caught Alice by the upper arms and gripped her.

“No!” she gasped. “Someone came? Did you see who it was?”

“It was the Master!” Alice laughed. “He must have been drinking at the Green Man last night and took the shortcut through the churchyard. I reckon he must have had a skinfull too, Mum, with his head down and staggering! Lucky he didn’t see me. I just nipped over the wall and ran all the way back to Mother and my little bed!”

“Are you sure it was John, the Master?” Mary asked, leaning back in bed.

"Oh, yes, Mum, though I thought it strange he was still wearing his old working jacket and farm boots. I supposed he'd gone on a whim, or maybe an errand in town, and been delayed… Mum, are you all right?"

Mary opened her eyes and gave a hollow smile. For she knew that when Alice thought that she had seen John chasing behind her in Ashbourne churchyard, he had been asleep beside her. She had sat, unsleeping for the kicks and movements of the baby inside her and had seen her husband head on the pillows by her elbow, and had heard his deep, untroubled breathing. Something else had happened, though…

She had lain in bed, with the warmth of her sleeping man's back against her, idly playing with her fortune-telling cards on the quilt over her knees, a single candle by her shoulder on a stand. Nothing, nothing, nothing. Cut, deal a spread, nothing. Ever since she had become pregnant, the cards had been dead to her. Again, nothing. She held the pack of brightly coloured cards with their strange pictures in her hand and leant back on the pillow. Why would the cards not speak? She had so much to ask them. She heard the first chimes of midnight, ringing up the dale from Saint Oswald's, and then she saw before her in the air something tiny, no bigger than a grain of mustard seed, but brightly shining, dart past, brushing her cheek like a moth drawn to a flame. It hovered a moment before darting toward the door and melting through it. Mary had blinked, shook her head. Absently she stroked her cheek where the little spark had passed so closely to her. She was tired, imagining things.

But that tiny spark of light she had seen must have been a fragment of John's living spirit, rising up, bright and fast as fairy dust, passing like lightning, summoned down the dale, down to Ashbourne to follow his future wife, which could only mean…

"Well, this won't buy the baby a new bonnet!" Mary said, putting on the best face she could and pretending to be happy. "Come, Alice, you go prepare the breakfast and I shall join you shortly."

"I'll stir the fire and get the kettle going, ma'am," said Alice. "It's a brisk day. We need to keep you warm."

"Aye, aye," said Mary, absent-mindedly.

Later, when the two women had eaten and Mary was sat by the huge kitchen range, she called to Alice and the young woman came bustling up to her with her arms all floury from the loaves she was kneading.

"I have another little love charm for you, my girl," Mary said. "Go to the door and take the big key out, then look straight through the keyhole and tell me the first thing that you see. No cheating, now, no squinting, or a cold wind will take you and set your face like that!"

The maid ran to the door and did as her mistress instructed. She took the key out of the big, old lock and put her eye to the keyhole to look out upon the path and the farmyard beyond.

"I don't see much, Mum," she said doubtfully, "Oh, those pesky hens again!"

"What do you see?" Mary asked.

"Why, they've got in the garden again, and they're pecking around! That old cockerel is chasing the brown hen again!" Alice laughed, then turned to see her mistress looking pale and wide-eyed at her.

"What is it, Mum?" Alice asked.

"Why," Mary said, recovering. "It's going to be quite a year you will have! For, if you had seen one person or a single creature', then that is how you would have remained till next Valentine's Day, single. If you had seen two or more people or things, then it would have meant that you would find a sweetheart this coming year. But to see a cock and hen, means you will marry before the year is out."

"Oh, Mum!" Alice laughed, returning to her baking, "There's not a chance of that. Besides, I wouldn't leave you till your baby's born and you are well again!"

No, thought Mary, but I may leave you, and you will marry the Master, my John. Slowly she walked upstairs, and taking out the old pack of cards, she cast them again, not for herself, but for the child she was carrying. And this time the cards spoke to her. They told her that the baby would be a girl, and all would be well with the child, but it did not mention Mary, not matter how many times she cast it.

And now Mary knew what she had to do before she died. She spent many hours talking inwardly to her baby, directing all her thoughts and energy, and the little spark of spirit within her went into the baby too, so strange, so that sometimes she felt that she was the baby and the baby spoke to her.

Mary died when the baby was born, and then, with John grief-stricken and lost to the world for weeks, the young Alice took over. She found a wet nurse for the baby, extra help in the house and fields until John recovered, and she nursed and cared for the beautiful child that Mary left behind and she loved it as her own.

There was a Christmas wedding in Ashbourne, and John brought his new wife home with pride and the best wishes of all who knew the couple. They said John deserved happiness after all he had been through, and the beautiful baby deserved a mother as good as Alice.

"There now, my dear little Mary," said Alice on the day after the wedding, settling by the fire with her precious bundle, "Now, soon you will talk and learn to call me Mum, but I shall still be the one who cares for you. What do you think of that, my little darling?"

And the baby looked up at its chosen mother with such dark and obsidian eyes, and it gave a familiar little chuckle that made Alice open her eyes with surprise.

"And hello to you too, my dear," Alice said when she had recovered. "And thank you for the gift."

AN IRISH MAID WOULD MARRY

The Irish were no strangers to the Peak as itinerant labourers and servants. Many Irish men and some Irish women would come over to England in the summer and work their way up the country, following the harvest and finishing off at Peak farms, or travelling even further north before taking their money home to their own little farms in the Emerald Isle. A lot of them were regular visitors, coming to the same place every year for as long as they were able. Some, particularly the domestic servants, would stay for longer. They were well liked and respected for their hard work and honesty in their dealings. On their annual arrival they were often eagerly greeted as they had become friends with those on the farm, and so there are some fond stories and short tales of them in Peak District lore. Some are so short they could be classified as jokes rather than tales, but then what is a joke but a short funny story? Here is one short tale.

A young Irishwoman called Eireen was working as a domestic servant on a large farm. Also working there as a labourer in the fields was a young Irishman called Padraig. He and Eireen fell for each other, and there was a proper courtship, with 'walking out' in the evening after work was done, flowers and small tokens of love and the whole rigmarole. Very few Irishmen are lost for words of flattery when they meet a woman they like, and Padraig was no exception. He won the heart of Eireen, and though she encouraged him, and as the months wore on, there was no mention of an engagement, or marriage. Both had contracted for a year's service with the farmer, and there was no guarantee that both would be retained when Martinmas came round, and the rehiring took place, nor had Padraig said whether he would stay on if asked to. It was all a worry for poor Eireen, and she decided to ask for spiritual assistance.

That posed a problem, however, for both Eireen and Padraig were Catholics, and there was no priest or Catholic church for many a mile. Eireen decided to go to the nearby woods to pray for divine intervention, where she could be alone and not seen or heard. Accordingly, the following Sunday she dressed in her best gown and bonnet as if going to church and crept out of the house really early and up the hill to the wood, unobserved. Reaching a hedge under a tree, she knelt on a grassy bank, lit a small candle she had brought in her bag, along with her rosary, and began to pray. When she had completed all her usual prayers she put her rosary in her pocket and addressed the Virgin Mary directly.

"Oh, Mary, Holy Mother of God," she prayed, clasping her hands tightly and with her eyes up to Heaven, "Please, please, please, can I have Padraig as my husband?"

Little did Eireen know that a tramp had slept the night nearby, under a bush in the woods and was somewhat tetchy and grouchy at being woken up so early. Can't blame the man; I'm the same myself. So, he sat up and said in a hollow voice, "No! Thou cans't not! Be off with you!"

And Eireen replied, "Hush thee, little Jesus, and let thy mother speak!"

THE PEDLAR AND THE DEVIL

The pedlar cursed softly to himself as he plodded on into the falling night. Rain clouds had appeared and a wind was getting up. He followed the cart track, which wound across the moors then descended sharply by the side of a sheer drop, to the racing brook below, and eventually he reached the highway where the going would be easier. Rain broke out; a chill wind whipped his face with cold drops of water buffeting the bulky oblong wood-and-canvas pack he was carrying on his back. He walked bent forward with the weight of it, supporting himself with a stout wooden staff secured to his wrist by a thick leather strap. After a half mile or so on the highway he paused, backing up to a drystone field wall and perching his load on its top. He pulled his long heavy coat around his body more tightly and continued cursing to himself, pausing occasionally to spit in disgust. Heavy clouds obscured what moon there would be, and travelling this night was going to be slow.

He cursed the farmer's wife at first. If auld Aggie Oates hadn't been so hungry for company, and kept him long past his time, gossiping and passing on the news he had gathered along the way from the isolated farms and villages he called

Taddington Vale, where the pedlar meets the devil at the crossroads

on, he'd have been close to Spitewinter Farm by now, snug and warm in Jack Meakin's barn this night, with a belly full of good rabbit or beef stew to boot. And the dumplings Jack's wife made! He groaned softly to himself and swore again.

But the farmer's wife had a good heart, he decided eventually, and had bought plenty from him, lightening his pack a good deal once he had passed over the items she had asked him to bring her when he had last called at the farm, nigh on harvest time. Beneath his layers of clothing, warm and safe, his purse was heavy with the silver coins she had paid him. A pair of Sheffield steel scissors, good and sharp, a small bolt of fine tweed all the way from Harris in his home country of Scotland (Ah! How he missed it this nicht!), fine Spanish sewing needles, pins from Gloucestershire, and half a dozen pewter buttons from London, cast with a stag's head design upon each one. All to make a fine waistcoat for Master Oates tae brace himsel' oot at the Christmas, he had thought to himself as Aggie clapped her hands in delight when he handed each item to her. Aye, she was a fine one with the needle. He had made her a present of a bobbin of thread with which to put it all together. Generosity was his failing mark, he told himself, as he recalled it now.

No, he could not curse her, he thought in his charity, he could not. It was a solitary and lonely life being a 'Scotchman' as the Derbyshire folk called all pedlars, whether they were from God's country or no, and he had been sore wanting company, light and laughter.

The rain began to bucket down, and in the hope that it was just a passing storm, he hurried across the road and half crawled with pack on back like some drab beetle under a cluster of hawthorn bushes. It was some shelter, though far from being enough for the coming night if this rain continued, for autumn was well advanced, and the leaves were fallen. His pack would be safe through any downpour, with its waterproofed double lining of oiled canvas buckled tight, but soon the water began to find its way beneath his clothing and within minutes he was damp and shivering.

So, not in all charity being able to curse Aggie Oates, he glumly decided to curse himself for his plight, wet and cold – aye and hungry too – sitting crouched like a sick bird under a bush, with the darkness like a bag around him.

'You're a dratted fool,' he told himself savagely, always one for a blether and mug of something. The light and warmth of the kitchen, the food and drink, had seduced him into staying longer than was wise, and now here he was, benighted. 'Ach, weel,' he said, 'as Granny used to say, what can't be cured must be endured.' Stupid, unfeeling sentiment, he thought sourly as he dragged his pack out and shouldered it, water coursing off its top and down inside his sleeve. She'd be greetin' her eyes oot, facing this! See what she'd ha' to say then!

He plodded on, feeling his way with his staff on the road before him. Derbyshire roads were notoriously bad. One man had even drowned in a hole in a Peakland road! No broken limbs for the pedlar, no spills and broken wares. Taddington Dale loomed before him, the mouth of the dale bearded with trees which grew up over the road and made it even darker and more treacherous. The hills rose up either side of the dale, and the River Wye rushed noisily past him, in high spate, drowning out any noise there might be of approaching danger.

And danger there was on the roads, he thought. If you did not trip and fall on an uneven surface or wander off course and fall over an edge or into the river, the roads in this wild county were known to be the hunting grounds for many a footpad and highwayman. A pedlar was good bounty for such as those, with his wee purse of gold and silver. And then, if they didn't find you, here in the dark, there were other beings who, they said, haunted the deserted byways of the Peak.

Such things as the boggart, the big, black dog which the locals swore was to be encountered in the lanes of Derbyshire, a spirit animal which blocked a traveller's way menacingly and would not allow one to pass, forcing a man to leave the road and become lost on the moors or in the woods, perchance meeting with an accident in the darkness. And, of course, at the crossroads – at any crossroads – high on the moors, it was said the devil would keep a rendezvous for those who wished to meet him there under the cover of darkness. One only had to pray for him to come. And when the devil came, the stories went, he would fulfil any wish asked of him, but he would always name his price, and the price was usually…

The pedlar shivered at the thought of evil waiting for him on the moorland crossroads above the dale he travelled through. Even the devil would not be out on a night like this, he thought, and he'd welcome even a devil's help this night, the pedlar reflected sourly. And even as the thought came that he had called upon the devil, he had a sudden, intimate feeling of something awakening, just as a dog lying asleep will stir itself, raise its head and sniff the air to ascertain what it is that woke it. The pedlar dispelled the notion and his earlier blasphemy with a swift prayer, for he was a staunch member of his kirk, who believed in the strength of the covenant he had made with God, and the power of his own prayers. Even so, his heart was in his mouth at every sudden lashing of a branch in the wind, the bark of a nearby fox in the wood, the splashes and gurgles of the Wye.

It was a weary pedlar who finally negotiated the last turn of the upward winding road and cleared the trees. A heavy mist still lay over the land, but the rain and wind began to lessen, and soon the traveller came out through the mist to see the moors above him lit by a bright, full moon and cold stars glittering in the heavens. Not a sign was there of anyone else on the road, nor any human habitation, where he might beg a night's rest.

It was then that he remembered passing this way in the daytime some months ago, and upon reaching the crossroads atop the moors had seen the old grey walls of a crumbling, ruined house in the distance, over towards Millers Dale and the Tideswell road. If he could just find shelter there among the ruins he could light a fire and dry off, even catch a few hours' sleep perhaps. He felt better already, being away from those dark woods and all the strange sounds that inhabited the cold, dripping depths. The rain dropped, and the young man's spirits lightened. After all, he thought, ye've had worse, mah mon! He began to whistle, an old jig he had often danced to, back home. The tune was a favourite one of his, 'The De'ils A mang th' Tailors'.

He was amazed when the tune was whistled back to him, from somewhere higher, toward the crossroads, and he heard a horse stamp and whinny. Caution halted his steps and he peered through the darkness, not sure whether to go on or to retreat the way he had come and find some sort of refuge in the woods below. He half-turned to look back the way he had come and saw something which brought the hairs on the back of his neck up in a bristle.

There, standing athwart the centre of the road, was a truly massive black dog, bigger than any mastiff or deer-coursing dog he had ever seen in his rambles through either Scotland or England. Its eyes shone green in the moonlight, and it regarded him unflinchingly.

"Could that be a boggart?" the pedlar asked himself and realised that he dare not, could not, retrace his steps. A boggart barred his retreat. Steep embankments on either side hedged with wild blackthorn trees ruled out any escape that way; there was no choice but to go on and face the whistling stranger at the crossroads. The pedlar tried to continue his jaunty whistle about the devil being among the tailors, but found his mouth too dry with fear to raise the slightest peep, and he recalled his earlier thoughts about the Dark One who waited at remote crossroads such as these before him to strike a bargain with the willing – or duped – traveller: the mortal's dearest wish fulfilled, in exchange for their immortal soul upon the time of their death.

"Oh, would that I were far and awa' fae here," the man moaned, "and hame safe with mah ain folk!"

But the Scots are a plucky race, and he hoiked his pack higher on his back and walked on, his staff now held like a sword before him, should something chance to rush out at him. He'd poke the foe backward, then drub them with the sturdy cudgel end of the stave. Aye, that's whut he wud dae!

Reaching the crossroad, he was relieved to see that the stranger was a stout old man in a farmer's smock and leather leggings, astride a very old and fat farm horse.

"Hail fellow, well met," the farmer greeted the pedlar jovially. "You'll be the Scotchman, name of Alan Urquahart, I trust? Eeeh, but ow looks wet, me lad!"

"How do you know my name?" asked Alan the pedlar.

The farmer beamed in the darkness and tapped the side of his large nose.

"There's not much gets past me, my boy," he chuckled. "Owd Nick Bradbury has all his chairs at wom! Yer carrying a pack, so you're a Scotchman, and youngest of the pedlars as comes rahnd 'ere is young Urquahart frum t' Bonnet Toun up in Scotland, Stewarton, I hear it's called, where they meck all them big floppy 'at's the Scotch like to wear, look a bit like Bakewell puddings! Am ah right?" He leant down from his saddle and offered his hand.

"Nick Bradbury's the name, Alan," he said, "and it's me pleasure to offer yer a night's lodgin' and a good meal into the bargain. Come on, me lad, let's get yer t' me farm an' get yer dry an' fed!"

Alan marvelled at the farmer knowing so much about him and felt lucky indeed that he had been waiting at the crossroads to offer him such hospitality. It was what he had been hoping and wishing for as he trudged up the dale.

"That was a fine tune you were whistling there,' old Bradbury commented as he guided Alan off down the road to Millers Dale, his horse ambling alongside the pedlar. "D'ust know what it's called?"

"Th' Dei'l's Amang th'Tailors, sir."

Nick laughed a strange deep laugh and said, "And well he might be, for they are thieving bunch of rascals, them tailors! However, they say that there are more clerics than tailors in Hell, don't y'know, but both are men of the cloth! Now, I knew the jig yer whistled, but not th' name. D'yer play music, young Alan, my lad?'

"Aye, that I do! I play the tin whistle. I've one in my pack the now."

"Then we shall ha' music as well as good food and drink tonight!" the farmer said happily, "For I play the fiddle, yer know! Hup there, Lilith! Oh, dunner mind 'er, me friend. She has an evil nature."

This last was to Alan as he made to hold onto the horse's bridle for support on the rough road. Although a mild-looking old nag, Lilith whipped her head sideways and tried to take off a few of his fingers with her large, yellow teeth. She cast the pedlar a baleful look out of one rolling eye, and for a moment Alan thought he saw a red light in its depths.

"Lilith? Tis a strange name for a horse, Maister Bradbury," observed Alan.

"Aye," said the farmer, "And an apt one too, methinks, for a horse in the Peak!"

"How?" asked the young pedlar.

"It says in the Bible, Isiah, I believe, that Lilith 'was a dweller in waste places," said the farmer, "An' as you have found this night, the Peak's a cold an' wet wilderness!"

"It is believed also that Lilith was Adam's first wife, and that she was a demon," said Alan, not wishing to argue, but feeling it was his duty as a religious man to object to levity where the Bible was concerned. "I was always taught that it is gey bad luck to name one's animals after people – or devils – in scripture."

"But, Alan," laughed the farmer, "Yer not in yer own country now, lad! We do things different! Ho, there! Herod! Stay!"

Bradbury had turned on his horse and was bellowing back down toward the crossroads. The corpse-white light of a full moon illuminated the figure of the boggart, slinking like a small, malevolent bear to seal off the turning down to the farmer's house.

"That is your dog, sir? Called Herod?" asked Alan.

"Aye, one of 'em," said the old farmer absently. "Come, me new-found friend; us'll dine well tergether in a warm, dry place!"

The pedlar decided not to mention the name of old Nick Bradbury's dog, but he remembered hearing once in Northumbria an old folk-belief that King Herod, by whose command an untold number of innocent babies was slaughtered, was condemned by God to wander the face of the earth in the shape of a black cur-dog until the end of time.

His morbid thoughts were banished as, breasting a rise, Alan could see below, where only crumbling ruins had been the last time he had passed that way, a well-built stone farmhouse from whose mullioned windows light brightly streamed. An open door shone further light out upon a gravelled drive as if to welcome the drenched and hungry pedlar. Alan's feet slurred with exhaustion as he trod upon the loose stones of the approach.

"I fancied the place to be an old ruin when I came this way a year back," he said.

"You are mistaken," the farmer said as he dismounted. "I have always been here." He handed his reins to a shadowy, hooded figure which bowed low as it took charge of Lilith and led her away through the rain to the stables at the side of the house.

Alan stepped inside the farmhouse with Nicholas's hand in the small of his back, guiding him deeper inside the old dwelling.

"Mind your step, my lad, 'tis uncommon dark in the passage here. We eat in the room before you. Lay your pack here in the hall and lift the latch, if you please."

Alan thought to himself how strange it was that, though light abounded as it came from the windows, there was little shown inside the house, and a morbid and unbidden thought came to him of a strong brilliance being shown to attract moths to the flame, where, trapped, they burnt helplessly in agony. Could this be a ruse of some sort?

He paused before the door, irresolute. Was it too late to turn back, to push past the stranger who claimed to be Nicholas Bradbury, a simple farmer, but whose presence behind him now raised the hair on the nape of his neck with foreboding? Even as he hesitated, the old man leant around Alan and snicked the latch, pushed open the door.

"Ladies and Gentles all, we have a friend to dine!" cried Nicholas, and pushed Alan through the door, into a shadowy dining room with a large, bare oaken table running down its length. Weak candles guttered on the table, the strongest illumination of the room coming from an outsize fire which blazed and roared in the inglenook stone fireplace, lighting up with a pulsing red wash the company assembled at the dinner table, who had all turned to look at Alan as he unwillingly entered.

And what a strange, sinister brood they seemed, the young pedlar thought as he looked upon what he could see of their flame-licked forms. They were indistinct, huddled over the table in shadows which clung to them. Here he saw a face, watchful, ugly, eyes glittering, there an arm, reaching out over the table to seize a wooden platter, and the noise of their shouting and imploring for more space at the table reminded Alan of pigs at a trough. He tried to focus, but the air itself in the close, hot room seemed to thicken and waver like a curtain in a breeze, so that the servitors who bustled past him with dishes and long, sharp knives which they laid on the table, kept changing in form, shrinking and expanding, but always hunched over, malformed and distorted. The very air contained forms, like bubbles in boiling fat, and something dropped from the ceiling upon the pedlar. He brushed at it and saw that little tears of red liquid that looked like blood were falling from the low ceiling of the room.

Alan thought that perhaps his sheer exhaustion and his exposure to such heat was turning his head, was causing him to hallucinate. His brow was wet with sweat, he wavered and almost fell but the strong arm of the old farmer was suddenly holding him up, a steel grip held his elbow and forced him forward to the head of the table.

The shadows around the figures at the table shrank and he could see the painted face of an old crone, her lank, once golden hair hanging like dry straw, the sweating jowls and dewlaps of a hugely obese old man in a wig, the cunning and diseased face, of a young dandy gambler, his velveteen coat and lace cuffs dirty and torn, cards in one trembling hand, here a man with ears clipped and the brand of a criminal impressed on his forehead, there a rat-faced man with an elongated neck which hung over to one side of his body a blackened tongue lolling and the impression of a hempen rope around his neck, all – and more – pressing forward, shoulder to shoulder around the table. The rain of blood drops became stronger, then the air wavered, and objects began forming in it, and dropping to the floor. Alan saw toads and slugs and beetles and other crawling things form and fall, then a spider, as large as a child's clenched fist, dropped onto his arm. He shook it off and it landed on the table among the plates and cutlery, kicking out its black, hairy legs. The hag stretched forth a bony claw and scooped up the spider with her yellowed dirty talons. She raised it to the side of her head and patted it into place on her hair, where it clung like some hideously carved jet ornament. Another hand, that of the hanged criminal, reached out and scraped the spider from her filthy hair and forced the wriggling creature past his cracked lips and blackened tongue, chomping down upon it.

"Extra meat!" croaked the hanged man hoarsely to the room at large, and there came a gale of insane laughter and shrieking which caused Alan to hold his hands over his ears in fright. What was happening to him? Had he caught a fever in the rain, was he suffering from some heat upon his brain? Was he really seeing all this, or was he imagining it? He thought that he might wake in a moment and see the farmer, his family and servants all ranged before him, about to take their supper in domestic harmony and looking concerned that their surprise guest was not well.

A strong hand came down upon Alan's arm and pushed him even further towards the table, until he was pinned against the heavy oaken slab. Closer now, he could see strange, dark stains and deep cuts upon its surface. It was Nicholas Bradbury who held Alan firmly and fixed the crowd with a stern glare.

"Gentles all!" the old farmer's voice cut like a whip over the mob's heads. There was an immediate, cowed silence. Bradbury nodded.

"Better," he said, sternly. "Let us not forget ourselves! Now…" he indicated Alan with another nod of the head, while continuing to hold him firmly. Alan was strong and wiry from carrying his heavy pack for miles across the Peak each day but was helpless in the old man's grip.

"Allow me to introduce and welcome our guest this even, Mister Alan Urquhart," Nicholas said, "a Scotchman both by trade and birth!" There was a murmur, stifled laughter, then the farmer said, "I sent you all out to find someone to invite to this feast, yet – again – it is I who come back bearing fruit. For shame, my children!"

"Master," whined one, "It is a foul night, and no one was astir, no one treading the Peakland roads."

Nicholas nodded. "Just a poor pedlar benighted, who sent a prayer out into the darkness, and I heard and went to his call. But come, we delay, let us eat!"

Nicholas clapped his hands and the twisted, deformed servitors scurried in with bowls for all, dishes of turnips and other vegetables, but no meat. The hugely fat man rose with difficulty and much groaning and panting and lumbered over to the hearth. He lowered a griddle on soot-blackened chains over the blazing fire, stirred the among the flames with a poker until there was a steady, glowing bed of hot coals.

The crowd around the table grew feverish in their

excitement. One called out that he wanted ribs, well charred, another wanted rump steak, well done, someone shouted for leg, done anyhow, and the crone mumbled that she would settle for trotters and knuckles, where the sweetest of meats was to be found. She looked at Alan and ran her tongue over her mean little mouth and sharp teeth.

"Hold hard, my good hosts!" shouted Alan the pedlar, breaking free of Bradbury's grasp. "Are we no forgetting a wee something?"

"What, what? Hungry, hungry," the assemblage screamed.

Alan took off his good Scotch bonnet and clasped it before him.

"I am but a poor Scottish pedlar," Alan began, "but I was received intae the kirk and learnt my catechism at my mother's knee. Now, I am no conversant wi' the ways o' you sassenachs here – nae offence y'ken – but speakin' for mysel', I cannae break bread without saying my grace and giving thanks tae the Lord for what he aye lays before me!"

Accordingly, he tucked his bonnet beneath his arm, clasped his hands together, and made to pray. It was the Kilmaurs grace which Alan used, an old prayer in good lallands scots, fragments of which only remain today.

"We gi' thanks in the name an' grace o'… o'," he stammered as the din around him increased and old Bradbury seized his arm and began to shake it. "We gi' oor thanks in the name an' grace o' the maister makar o' heaven an' all below, to God oor father and his braw son…" began Alan.

"No! No! Noooo!" screamed Nicholas, "Forebear, Scotchman!" and the others around the table began to moan and caterwaul in fear.

"Jesus Christe, wha cam immaculate intae this world o' sin…" Something foul swept out of the fireplace and enveloped Alan in a fog of sulphur and the smell of roasting flesh, and he realised that the almost unbearable shrieking that nigh deafened him was coming from the fireplace as if from the depths of hell, but he battled on. "For tae deliver us a' fae a' evil…"

It was as if a giant hand folded itself around Alan and shielded him, and another one smote the house, so that with a great roar the walls buckled and collapsed, the floor heaved beneath them all and the roof caved in around them. A soft, sweet breath with the power of a gale swept over the place and the evil crew around the table were plucked up and thrown into the black sky like autumn leaves, screaming as they went into the void.

"Lilith!" bellowed Nicholas, old Nick, and his horse appeared at his side, changing into the she-demon of the Old Testament as she came. Weeping and screaming in anger, she plucked Nick up, and rose gibbering skyward and away, followed by the black boggart Herod, whose shape was now his truer one, that of the cruel, child-murdering king of old. Condemned by their iniquities and bound for those sins to Satan for eternity, they served him as ever and vanished upward into the night sky. One sudden spark that flared then died, and they were gone.

Alan fainted to the floor of the old house, his last sight being Nick's hairy haunches bending and springing upward towards Lilith, and his smoking cloven goat's hoof close to Alan's head pressing down on something on the floor, something wet which sizzled and stank of smouldering wool.

When Alan awoke it was dawn. The sun shone, and sweet birds sang in the clean morning air. He sat up unharmed and looked around him, at the ruined farmhouse with moss growing over the capsized roof and mouldering thatch, the great roof timbers decayed to pulpy fingers pointing through the lichened building stones where walls had been only the previous night. A venerable oak tree grew in the midst of the ruin. Clearly it was many a year since the farm had been lived in – by any mortal being. Somewhere, Alan thought, beneath all that rubble, lay his pack. No matter, he still had his purse and his good staff; he was done with the peddling life.

He had all that he needed. He looked toward the sun to gauge West, then he set his face North and struck out for fair, far Caledonia and home. If he set a good pace, he thought, he could be home in two weeks or so, never to return.

True to his resolve, Alan Urquahart, pedlar, never did return to the Peak, nor did he become a pedlar again. If anyone asked him why he gave up the pedlar's life and took to being a cobbler in old Stewarton village, with a good wife and his wee, white Ayrshire cottage filled to the brim with children, he would say his wandering days were done, or some such excuse. Only to a favoured few would he tell the tale of how he once met the devil at a moorland crossroads in the Peak of Derbyshire one foul night, and narrowly escaped being eaten and his soul forfeit for calling up the devil. And if any scoffed, or said he merely fell asleep in some old ruins and dreamed it all, Alan the one-time 'Scotchman', the pedlar, would open a cupboard by the fireside of his cottage and take out an old and worn Stewarton blue bonnet with a red 'toorie' or pom-pom on it, and, turning the hat over, would show the astounded visitor, inside the bonnet the clear brand scorched into the wool of a cloven hoof, a hoof print like the hoof of a goat – or Old Nick.

FAIRY PIPES

If you garden in the Peak or explore its old lead mines, chances are you will come across fragments of old, clay tobacco pipes lying in the soil of your garden or on the floor of the mine, usually the stems, as the smoker would discard the pieces of stem which broke off and keep smoking until the warmth of the smokers' nose indicated buying another pipe. It was the tobacco which was dear; the pipes were cheap, were even given away in some local taverns to attract more custom. These fragments are not peculiar to the Peak; they are to be found the length and breadth of these islands, but in the Peak they had a special name: Fairy Pipes.

So small were the bowls, and so strong the belief in fairies at one time in the Peak District, that many countryfolk (or 'Peakrels' as the Victorian antiquarians fancifully called them!) believed that the pipes had belonged to the little people, and possessed magical properties of their own, long after the fairies had lost or discarded them.

One story which was commonly told in the Peak District, names and small details changed with the area and teller of the tale, was that of a farm labourer who found a pipe as he ploughed a field. It was in a good condition, with bowl intact and a good length of stem, so he took a seat on a nearby grassy bank, carefully cleaned out the bowl with his knife, and filling it with a few pinches of tobacco, sat down to enjoy a quiet, contemplative smoke before resuming work.

The tobacco in the pipe burnt so sweetly; the smoke wasn't hot, as a good length of stem was still attached, and the tobacco even tasted different to when the ploughman had smoked it in his regular clay pipe. He refilled the pipe after it had burnt out, tamped the tobacco down, scraped a lucifer into life against the stone wall above his grassy bank and lighted his new pipe, and inhaled deeply with the sheer pleasure of the true nicotine addict. But this time it had a different, strange effect upon him. His eyes began to smart and tingle; his vision swam so badly that he put one hand out to steady himself, even though he was seated, and found that he could not feel the ground beneath him. Looking upward, he could not see the sun. He felt breathless and blew in and out rapidly to get his breath back and, dropping his head, he saw to his amazement that he could see through the solid ground that lay before him!

Beneath a large, oblong stone which had lain, half-buried, at one side of the field since he could remember, and before his grandfather, who had been a ploughman too, said he could remember, the surprised labourer could see a whole elfin world of beautiful trees with jewelled leaves and blossoms, birds of exquisite plumage like none he had seen in his world flying in and out of them, flowing crystal streams which glittered their way through emerald meadows past delicate, pastel-coloured fairy castles whose flowing architecture made it seem as if they had grown from the fragrant ground, rather than being built from cold, dead stone. And through this enchanting scene moved scores of tiny people dressed in the brightest of gowns and cloaks and capes and hose from a time long past on this earth. And as they moved through this scene they sang and played on tiny instruments the most sweet music he had ever heard, all untroubled and untouched by the troubles of the human world above them.

Carefully, the ploughman put his pipe safely in a deep jacket pocket, wrapped in a soft kerchief. He kept his magic pipe for many years, and when he felt sad or sick at heart with the ways of men, he would take his elfin pipe and some tobacco, and walk up to the old stone in his master's field, and smoke awhile, and watch the doings in a better world than that which man has built for himself.

A less charming tale survives, being that of a man who was digging in his garden and who found one of the fairy pipes with bowl intact. Stooping to pick it up, he saw a tiny old man dressed in green, the favourite colour of fairies and 'fey' folk, including witches. The little old man was sitting on the stem of the pipe, swinging his legs and scowling at the man. The man blinked and rubbed his eyes with his free hand, bent his head a shade closer to take a better look. The little elf jumped up and ran along the stem of the pipe and stood in the bowl of it, from where he took up an aggressive stance and made threatening gestures at the gardener, whilst pulling the most frightening of faces! So terrified was the man that he dropped the pipe onto the soft soil which he had just been digging, and turned away. When he looked back, the pipe and its tiny owner had disappeared, and though he searched all through the garden he could not find the pipe or elf, nor did he ever see them again.

Elfin pipes turned up quite frequently in old lead mine workings too, where 'the old man', the early leadminers, had discarded or lost them, and it was a belief that the fairies wreaked a swift revenge on anyone who stole their property. The Peak historian Llewellynn Jewitt who lived in the nineteenth century, wrote of one such instance where a lead miner on Brassington Moor found a fairy pipe when working below ground, and put it in his waistcoat pocket to give it later to Jewitt. It had not been long in his pocket, and he had resumed working, when he felt a most painful pricking to that side of his body where the pipe was stowed, like a bee sting or adder's bite, so he turned out his pockets and looked inside his shirt to see what it could be. He found nothing and feeling puzzled he put his few possessions back in his pocket to resume working, absent-mindedly placing the pipe back on the other side of his waistcoat, whereupon the little sharp stabbing pains started to torment him on that side instead!

At this, the miner took the pipe out of his waistcoat pocket and put it in the pocket of his jacket, which was hanging nearby. Later, when his shift of work was done and he came to put his coat on, he found that his pocket was smouldering, although he had no matches on him, and had not smoked all day. Even stranger, the pipe had disappeared, having burnt right through his pocket and melted into thin air!

Another lead miner, Jewitt reported, found a fairy pipe and, charging it with tobacco, sat down in his mine to enjoy a quiet smoke and see how the pipe suited him, whether it was a hot burning pipe or a nice, cool smoke. He lit it up and blew out a long plume of blue smoke before him in the still air of the mine. Suddenly he saw in disbelief a whole horde of tiny, winged fairies who filled the air around him, and bit and scratched him, or stuck into him tiny darts and lances which they carried and used with great skill. Finding them worse than a nest of disturbed hornets, the miner threw the pipe down to beat the fairies off, at which they swooped down on what was their pipe as it fell and carried it off, while the miner wished it, and its owners a very good riddance!

Not all the stories held that the pipes brought ill-luck, however, for in some places in the Peak the pipes were carried on the person as good luck charms. Jewitt knew of one man who had treasured such a pipe for many years, and when asked if he wished to part for it, the man declared stoutly, in broad Derbyshire, "Nay ar'd part wi a towth (tooth) sowner!"

So, if you do find such a pipe, be warned: examine it closely before lighting up, as there may be a government 'elf' warning printed on it!

THE FOOL AND THE FEBERRY TREE

Once there was a man, a very wealthy farmer, who although he was rich remained humble and simple in his ways. Quietly and without arrogant display he tried to follow the teachings of his faith, which said that pride was a sin, forgiveness of those who trespassed against one a duty, and that we were all placed upon this earth to care each for the other. In this way, all who knew the man loved him, and none came away from meeting him without feeling the better for it. His servants in his house, his labourers in his fields, were all well treated, and all grew old in his service, not wanting to leave him, for a good master was harder to find – and worth more – than gold.

Almost as if, like Job, he was being tried in his beliefs, the master was sent one day a very simple fellow by the name of Nicorbore, a shambling, ragged beanpole, as gaunt and ill-kempt as a scarecrow. There were some in the master's household – mainly one jealous, spiteful servant – who said that the resemblance did not end there either, that Nicorbore had been blessed too with the head of a scarecrow, for his poor noggin was as much use to him as a turnip, so slow of wit was he.

The rich farmer took pity on Nicorbore, sensing that he

had been ill-used by the world. He gave him new clothes to wear, three good meals a day, and a job as a servant in his household, but soon Nicorbore's clumsiness had even his kindly and forebearing master in despair, for Nicorbore broke the pots and spilled the ale, and when he was sent by the cook to draw water from the well, he dropped the water-pail down the well shaft without fastening it to the rope on the windlass first, and then nearly fell down the well himself in trying to retrieve it.

"In truth th'art a clumsy 'un, Nick, my lad," sighed Nicorbore's master, peering down the well. "That's a good pail gone, lost in th' watter, look thee!"

"Nay, mester," Nicorbore drawled. "Look dahn there. There's a couple of chaps down at th' bottom. Happen they'll look fer it, if'n we as ask 'em. Th' owd feller 'as a kindly face, look yer!"

"Yon's our reflections, yer grett lummock!" his master laughed, but gently. "Ah, well, yer too blunderin' ter keep in th' 'ouse, so get thee dahn to th' field by th' wood, and keep th' crows out on th' young corn, wilt?

"Ar, mester," Nicorbore said, brightening. "Ar'll do it rate nah, er sooner!"

So off he went, and the master busied himself with the loves of his life, his pig and his hounds, which he kept in finer sties and kennels than the 'rooms' in which most other landed gentry kept their servants. He was just coming back up the farm yard an hour or so later when he saw Nicorbore returning from the fields.

"What th' farraps!" the master exclaimed. "Didna ar tell thee ter go dahn cornfield and kape crows aht?"

"Ar, Mester," said Nicorbore, beaming with pride at having done a job right for once. "Ar've dun it, an' come back ter see what yer want dun next."

"I meant fer yer ter stay theer all dee!" his master said, exasperatedly.

"Didna nade ter," said Nicorbore, grinning lopsidedly. "Ar druv all crows aht er field, then shut both gates tight. They'll none gerrin nah!"

"Eeh, lad," the master said shaking his head and chuckling. "Is there owt tha's good at?"

Nicorbore hemmed and hawed to himself and dragged a foot in the dirt to help him think. "I like dogs, Mester," he said, eventually. "Way gerron well tergither!"

"Dus't?" beamed the master. "Well, gerroff down th' yard, and look after young Rosebay. Shay's whelpin' soon, an' it's 'er fost litter. Ah'll be dahn theer direckly."

Walking down the yard later, with a bowl of tater peelings for his favourite sow, who had just farrowed, the master saw Nicorbore, not in the kennels but standing in the sow's pen. He had a large bucket of water at his feet, and was about to drown the piglets, who were squealing loudly.

"Catapikins!" shouted the farmer. "Howd thy foot up! What art doin' lad?"

"Arm drownin' em, Mester," Nicorbore said, looking sorrowfully at the struggling piglet he held in his hands. "It's best wi' young 'ounds as are born prick-eared. Their ears should bay droopin', like. They'll none do any good when they full grown."

"Them's prize pigs yer in among!" the farmer spluttered. "Gerrout er theer!"

Many a man would have got shut of Nicorbore then and there, but the master was a kindly man, and in an odd way the simple young fellow seemed to brighten the place up by his presence, for there was no guessing what he would say

– or do! In time, Master became quite proud of Nicorbore, and would show him off to guests and repeat with glee the latest tale about him. Nicorbore had a slightly off-centre way of looking at things, and an approach to his tasks that could not be predicted, but he was enjoyable or amusing to observe, the master maintained. Occasionally, guests would seek Nicorbore out and give him small gifts of money for adding to the pleasure of their stay.

On one occasion a very important man came to stay, and Master decided before the man came to warn Nicorbore not to mention an unfortunate physical characteristic of the visitor.

"'E's gorra big nose, Nicorbore," he told his servant. "Poor feller's probably sensitive abaht it, so dunna say owt, 'ear?"

Nicorbore nodded vigorously and promised to keep mum about it. He kept his word too, but whenever the guest was nearby he would stare, transfixed by such a large proboscis. Eventually the man noticed, and said to Nicorbore, "Come, my man, what is it? A penny for your thoughts!"

"Nay, sire," Nicorbore replied earnestly. "Ar munner tell yer me thoughts. Master said as 'ow ar wonner ter mention thy grett snout!"

Far from being angry, the visitor was delighted, and told everybody the tale. When he came to leave, he gave Nicorbore a silver sixpence, telling Nicorbore that his thought had been worth more than a penny.

"Now hang on to that coin, my man," he said, "And it will grow. That's how I started!"

Nicorbore wondered aloud in the kitchen how one could make money grow, and a jealous and spiteful manservant in the house decided that he would have some fun at poor Nicorbore's expense.

"I hear tell that if you plant a coin under a feberry tree, it'll grow in the moonlight," he told Nicorbore slyly when he had him on his own. "Only you must tell no one or the charm won't work."

For the rest of the day, the servant watched the gooseberry bushes, or feberry trees as they are also known, and sure enough, just as dusk was falling he saw Nicorbore walk as nonchalantly as he could manage into the gardens at the back of the house, and stoop down by a particular gooseberry bush growing in a corner. When Nicorbore had left, whistling innocently, the servant crept into the garden, dug up the sixpence, and put a silver shilling in its place.

On the next morning Nicorbore was delighted to discover that his money really had grown overnight, doubling in value. Then a thought struck him.

"I'll leave thee another day," he said to the shilling in his palm, "An' 'appen tha'll grow some more."

From a hiding place the servant heard Nicorbore's innocent words and, laughing nastily, he resolved to take the cruel hoax a little further.

The next day Nicorbore returned to the feberry tree to discover that his shilling had grown into a whole half crown, worth two shillings and sixpence. Why, this was more profitable than growing gooseberries and selling them on the market! Hoping that his silver would grow further, he reburied the half crown and sure enough, when the sun rose on the following day, and Nicorbore dug beneath the feberry tree, the half crown he had left there had been replaced by a large silver crown piece, ten times the value of the original sixpence he had originally planted. With hopes of a golden sovereign the following morn, he placed it back in its own strange little seed bed, left furtively, and went to sleep that night in his room above the stables, dreaming of the wealth that would be his ere summer was out.

But the spiteful servant had grown tired of the teasing and wanted to torment Nicorbore even more cruelly. The crown had shrunk on the next day to a four-shilling piece and gradually, day by day, the value of Nicorbore's moonlight crop declined, until early one morning the poor fellow dug up a coin which was only half of the original sixpence, a tiny, threepenny piece, commonly called a 'joey'.

Nicorbore looked long at the tiny coin in his pocket, reproaching himself for his greed, then he remarked sadly to it, before slipping it into his waistcoat pocket, "Ar'll kape thee in there from nah on, afore tha shrinks away all together!"

The spiteful servant was delighted with his cruel trick. Not only had he enjoyed days of malicious fun, but he had also made a profit! He found it so amusing and thought that he had been so artful that he could not resist boasting about it to the other servants in the kitchen, and the master eventually was told about it. He sent directly for the cruel servant.

"By… but yer a grett, hulkin' lout, a… a… a… gorby!" he roared. "An' ah'd tonn thee aht on th' road rate nah, but it's not in me nature! Yer knows as the poor feller's pate is filled wi' nowt but scrattlecake, an' yow teased him merciless!"

"Ah'll gi 'im back the tanner," snivelled the servant.

"Ar, rate yow will! An' yow'll let 'im kape the joey, an' all," the farmer said. "An' just remember worrit sez in the good book about 'ayin' the mind an' 'eart o' a child if yer wanner gerrinter 'eaven. Young Nicorbore is sure er salvation, wi' a simple soul like 'is. There's norra wicked bone in the man. Are yow s'sure er bein' saved? Are any on us, eh? Now, think on!"

Nicorbore was given his money back by a repentant servant, with the threepence interest as ordered, as well as an apology, but it is not known whether he heard or understood the cruel trick played upon him, for although he stayed for the rest of his life with 'Mester', and worked hard and well in his garden and fields, it was always noticed that Nicorbore would have nothing to do with tending the feberry tree, and that he always shot it a sideways, suspicious glance as he passed it.

A GREAT DISTURBANCE

Snow had been falling since early Monday morning all over the Peak, borne on the fleet wings of a cutting North-easterly wind which scoured the dale (or the Delph, as locals called it). At first the flakes were small, sharp-edged, crystal little blades of ice which, carried in gusts, stung the face and numbed ungloved hands, were driven between folds of coats and under head shawls, blew under doorsills and stuccoed the outer walls of the old limestone cottages in the village. It drove the villagers who had no pressing business outside to the comforts of a warm hearth. By noon the powder snow had changed to large flakes as the wind dropped a smidgeon, great, goose-down white feathers which began to blanket the village and block the roads with lazy drifts, so that soon idleness from daily toil was enforced for most, save those who worked a loom in their cottage or made the boots and shoes the village was known for. By dark of night, the lanes were so clogged with drifts that no one could enter or leave the little settlement.

It was a select few who battled their way to the inn through the snow that night, six men in all, greeted as they entered by the landlord Tobias Hill, truly mine jovial host, since his even temper and booming laughter were known to all who gathered that night under his roof, around a blazing fire, each man with a full pot of ale, brewed to perfection and kept to its best by Tobias and his aged grandfather, Zadok, once the village blacksmith.

Having served all, Tobias carefully and with much show of respect brought in Zadok and seated him a wing chair in a warm ("but not where I'll roast, now, lad!") corner close by the other men, with a good Derbyshire wool blanket over his knees.

"I'll give us a toast, my lads!" said Peter Thornton, the wag of the party and the youngest, in his twenties still, his round shaven face yet reflecting a boyhood he had reluctantly abandoned. He was known for his ruses and foolery and enlivened any company he sat down among. Now he raised his pot of ale and cried out, "Here's to Saint Tuesday, lesser-known brother of Saint Monday, and I pray to that holy and beneficent one, that we might spend it as we do now, around a warm fire, in good company with such fine ale before us. Now join me in a hearty amen, my friends!"

"Nay," said Wat Whysall, a stick of misery, with a long sad face and a sparse red beard, who could always be relied upon to see the worst in anything. "If I don't work I see no wages, and then where shall I be? Calver Work'uss, that's where! Now then."

Peter laughed and shook his head reprovingly. "Wat," he chided, "I wish I had threepence less than thee, for if so, I should be on a par wi' Duke of Devonshire in his little cottage at Chatsworth."

There was general laughter then, for everyone was aware how close with his purse was Wat Whysall. It was known by all present that though he earned fair money lead mining up on the Edge above the village, he spent little and begrudged that which he had to. When Peter had started 'walking out' with a kitchen maid up at the Hall, Wat had remarked sourly, "Ar, and now ye'll find out as a penny bun costs tuppence!" and Peter had said, "That's as may be, Wat, me owd lad, but for tuppence y'get icing on your bun, if you catch me drift!" And he had winked slowly at Wat and asked the sworn bachelor innocently, "Ever eaten a nice, iced bun, Wat? No? I thought not. You get a lot for another penny, y'know! Y'should try it!"

The gathered men had laughed loud and long, while Wat turned red and glowered at a smiling Peter. That had settled Wat for that time, but since that day Wat had borne Peter a grudge, and Peter had resented the wet blanket which Wat's miserly attitude and comments often brought to quench the merriment of the little group, and so Peter the joker never missed a chance to 'take a poke' at the older man.

Peter's dislike of Wat showed one day when the group was met around the table by the fire, and Wat, for some reason, was absent. Hal Burrows, a silk weaver who lived a stone's throw from the inn, had commented on Wat's tightness with money, commenting that Wat could "squeeze a farthing so hard that the head o' the coin cried out for mercy!"

"Nay, nay, Hal," Peter had said sorrowfully, shaking his head, as if Hal were being too judgemental. "The man's but frugal. Aye, and for a purpose, a noble one, if you but knew it. You slander the man, my friend."

"Why, what's his purpose for being so mean?" asked Hal innocently.

"Weeeel…" Peter had said, putting his pot down and leaning forward conspiratorially toward the rest of the group, as if imparting a great secret of state. The rest of the group leaned in too, eager for a choice nugget of gossip, forgetting that this was Peter telling them.

"I have it on the sworn word of the parson that Wat, our noble and misjudged friend, is laying by him every penny he can scrimp together, so that his parents may marry some day!"

There was a howl of laughter, followed by a huge boom of hilarity from Tobias.

"Oh, Peterkin," the landlord had said, "that's the most pleasant way I've ever heard someone say something so cruel." He filled Peter's pot in appreciation. Peter was no fool.

"Threepence less than me?" grumbled Wat now, taking a sparing sip at his pint, a pint which he aimed to make last him the night. "And you had threepence less than I, then it's you would be in the work 'uss, and out of my hair. I'm but a poor, working man, not a wealthy duke as lives off the fat of the land. I say again, if that snow don't stop and I can't go to my work down the mine, then I don't earn. Then where shall I be?"

There came a wheezing laugh from Zadok in his corner chair.

"He has you there, Petey," said Zadok, "Wat answered well, but I'll tell you summat, Wat. If that snow kept me from going down the mine, I shouldn't care if it snowed for a year or more. I had my fill of that game as a young 'un."

Even at a very advanced age, Zadok, was still a big man, barrel-chested, and with wide shoulders and hands like hams. A life's time of working as the village blacksmith had turned a big man into a giant. His actual age no one in the village could say for sure, because Zadok wouldn't tell them. It was one of his little conceits to keep that to himself, and even Peter could not draw it out of the old man.

"Yous'll find it out when the mason comes to carve it on

my headstone," Zadok had told him sourly.

"Arr, but then you might be lying twice to us all," Peter had retorted swiftly, "Once under the stone, and once upon it!"

Zadok had cracked a smile but kept his secret.

"Aye, I had my fill of that game," Zadok repeated. "I always hated it, going down there in the dark. Imagine a great lump like me, stuck in one of those narrow seams, or squeezing through the ways they cut to get to the ore. Even as a young 'un I was big, and the other fellers used to chaff me, called me 'Corky', 'cos I were like a cork in a bottle!"

The men laughed dutifully, and Zadok was quiet for a while, his great, age-freckled bald head slowly fell forward until his chin was on his chest, and for a while it seemed that he slumbered, then he stirred and raised himself in his chair and resettled, drained his pot of ale and looked into the flames of the fire.

"I shall never forget my last day down a leadmine," he said, "Nor the date, the first day of November in 1755, and that will stick in my mind for ever. I was just a lad, and working in the Great Cucklett mine, and that was the day that I learned something the King in London didn't know about for two whole days, nor his government, no, nor all the clever men in Oxford and Cambridge. Now then."

"Seventeen fifty-five?" Peter broke in, calculating swiftly. "But, even if you were a boy in seventeen fifty-five that would make you..."

Old Zadok looked directly at Peter and said with a smile, "Very, very old, eh, Peter? And I wasn't a boy, I was a big lad, a youth, by rights a man, I suppose. So, think on that." He turned back to the group. "They called that mine the Never Fear before it became the Great Cucklett. Never Fear! That day I wasn't just afeared. I was terrified, terrified for my life, and my sanity too. I thought I would lose my reason."

Tobias reached over and took his grandfather's pot and went to refill it for him.

"Tell, them, gran'fer," he called from the far room where the barrels were kept on cold stone thralls. "It's a story worth telling."

"Well," said Zadok, "I fair loathed it down there, I'll tell you plain. I wasn't built for it, and I hated the walls, so tight they were to my shoulders, and being six hundred feet below the surface, wi' solid rock pressing down over my head. I felt hemmed in, like a bug ready to be crushed. The other men called me Corky, and that's what it felt like, being a piece of cork, wedged in the neck of a bottle. I was forever banging my nut and scraping my shoulders and elbows in tight spots and low passageways. Putting me down a leadmine was like putting a bulldog in a bird cage. The other men, a great bunch of lads, said that I would get stuck one day, they'd have to starve me for a wick or two to free me. They said, dunner worry, Zade, us'll throw a horse blanket over thee when we quit for the night!"

The others laughed at the idea. Tobias handed over the pot and his grandfather drank deeply and lapsed into silence, staring into the fire as he recalled that day so long ago.

"So... what was it you heard of before the King in London, Zadok?" asked Timothy Wheatcroft, parish clerk and village tailor, who in secret was writing a history of the village and welcomed all of Zadok's stories as grist to the mill.

"Now, hold your foot up, Timothy, my lad. I'm getting there," Zadok said tetchily, then he began, without looking up at his audience.

"I shall always remember the day because I thought

it was going to be my last on this earth," Zadok said. "It was the morning – about eleven of the clock – of Saturday November the first, All Saints' Day…"

He trailed off again and stared into the fire, and his audience waited patiently, whilst some of them did some mental reckoning as to the old man's age.

"I was coming down a gallery pushing an empty wagon. I'd been set to drawing ore to the winding shaft. I could hear the working gang shouting to each other," he resumed. "We were cutting a vein down the Great Cucklett. It was a vein they'd chased for some years, and when they found it, it was of exceeding quantity. It was a vein they cut at for more than two miles. It kept going down until they hit water and could go no further. Cut a sough to take the water away, but it wasn't sufficient to drain any lower. That was long after I got out of mining… Anyway, I was just coming back as I say, and I could hear the gang shouting to each other and then…"

"What, Master Hill, what?" Peter implored. He loved a good story and was on the edge of his stool.

"The solid ground began to move beneath me," Zadok said slowly, turning his gaze upon each man in turn, almost challenging them, as if defying anyone to scoff or belittle him. "It was as if I was drunk and couldn't find my feet. Another man who was down there later said it was like being on a boat, but I've never been on one in my life, either sea or inland. It bucked and swayed, aye, and the walls seemed to ripple. I was in some giant's hand, and he did with me as he would. It was, it was… unreal: walls and floor of solid limestone, six hundred feet down, moving it seemed like curtains in a wind. I turned to run, but… where to? I cried out and then I began to shake with fear so much that I dropped my light and was in total darkness. And then the sounds began."

Zadok seemed as gripped by the moment as the listeners were. No one spoke; all waited until it seemed right to carry on. Some of the group must have felt themselves to be down the Great Cucklett all those years ago, in a different century, for two or three drew their stools nearer to the fire and the reassuring presence of the others.

"The sounds were like nothing I'd ever heard before," said Zadok, "They were… terrifying, and I wasn't a lad to scare so easily, upon my word. But there came a huge groaning, as if some huge, trapped beast were crying out in its torment, suffering unto death, and there were huge explosions, like cannon firing, and the worst, the very worst…"

Zadok gave an involuntary shiver and twitch, "The worst was this sort of cracking, galloping sound like a great charge of horses or sharp-hooved devils racing towards us all, trapped down there. Then they swept all around and past me, and came the groaning again, and the earth moving around me too, moving as easy as water in a brook."

"My soul!" breathed Peter softly. "In God's name, what was it?"

"It was a terrible earthquake, like nothing ever known in Europe before, or since," Zadok said solemnly. "It started, they say, way out at sea in the Atlantic, and hit the Portuguese city of Lisbon, which is on the coast, a port city. It's an old city, an important one, and with it being a saint's day, and them all being papists, they were mainly in the cathedral and their other beautiful old churches, and those buildings all being hundreds of years old, the earthquake seized them and threw them to the ground with the people in them, and hundreds were crushed to death beneath the stonework."

"How terrible!" said Hal Burrows, taking reassurance in his own personal safety with a large draught from his pot of ale.

"Oh, that were just the start of it," Zadok said shortly. "Because it was a special day, they had all the candles lit and decorations up, and the fallen candles set ablaze to the whole mess, and that spread to the entire city till it was all aflame, burned for five days, they say."

"Poor souls," someone said.

"It don't even stop there, though you would have thought as that would have been more than enough," said Zadok, leaning forward in his chair, the candlelight in the tavern room reflecting off his bald pate. "The people who escaped rushed from the flames and whatnot to an open space where they thought they were safe. That was the docks. They massed there in a great assemblage, and then…" he paused for effect and looked around him, drawing the men closer into the story. "And then, they say a great wave came a-barrelling in from the open sea and came ashore, thirty feet or more high it was, thirty feet, imagine that! It broke on the dockside and came rushing inland like a great monster, carrying all before it and moving as speedily as a galloping horse, then turned back, carrying the broken and whole bodies alike back into the ocean, and out to sea, beyond reach or rescue, if there had been anyone able."

"How many died, in all?" asked old James Alan, bootmaker in the village, bent of body after a long life spent crouching over his cobbler's last, rising to buy another drink, and his bowed, crooked shape was caught up in the flicker of firelight and the dance of the candlelight and thrown up against the wall and low ceiling of the taproom, making a dark question mark of a shadow.

Zadok blew out his cheeks. "Thousands and thousands,

James," he said sadly, and shook his head. "No one rightly knew. The vicar who was here in the village then, he used to have a London news journal come by the mail coach each week, and he passed on to me pieces as dealt with that terrible day. I could read it, see? I'd had my schooling! Some bodies put it at several thousand, some at thirty thousand, others as high as eighty thousand all told. Whole families were lost, whole parts of the city disappeared. Who was to say where they went? Some may have fled, but it was as if a huge hand came down and took a large part of the place. That huge wave, they say, came in and out three times, as if to make sure it had taken all it could. They were gone from the land, and none spoke of them, none mourned or missed them, for there were none to do so. And there was many, many a one received no decent Christian burial, and their bones lie with the fishes even now."

"And on a holy day, as well," said Dickon Morris, a waggoner, his large paw of a hand nigh smothering his pint pot.

"I'll tell you summat else, an' all," said Zadok. "That huge shaking of the earthquake that passed through us down there was felt up top as well, all through this land, for in those papers the vicar brought me it said that all the big bodies of water in England and Wales, lakes and such like, showed a 'great agitation' upon their surfaces, waves where there were no tides to have caused them. I'll never forget that, a 'great agitation', for that's what I went through, down there in the dark, thinking every moment was going to be my last, or worst, that the passage I was in would close around me, and I would die slowly in the darkness, alone."

Zadok shivered slightly and held out his hands to the fire for the warming comfort of the blazing logs.

"After a while, a few minutes," he said, speaking very slowly with pauses as he relived that day. "After a while, one of the men came and found me. I never can remember who it was, but he was being calm as he could. 'Come on, lad,' he says to me, like he was gentling a horse, and he had a light, and he took me to the other men, and we went at a pace into the middle of the mine, where there was a large cavern, and we waited it out, each minute praying it would cease, while thinking this would be our grave. Twenty minutes or so it lasted, and there were five of those shakes and infernal noises after, so that each time we thought there would be a great one to finally bring the walls and ceilings down upon us, and after each one an awful stillness and deep silence, and it was the silence which nigh unmanned me. Then it stopped, just like that, and we were spared.

"We made our way back up the passages and drifts, and had to pick our way over great loads of mineral that had fallen from the sides of the mine, and the roof, and were amazed to find that the shafts remained entire and safe, and so at last we came back up on to God's green earth, and there, not far from the mouth of the shaft, we could see the earth all torn up, and there was a cleft in the soil about one hundred and fifty feet in length, a chasm you could call it, even, looking to me at the time as if all the devils which had afflicted us down there had burst free from the depths and rushed away to do their master's bidding elsewhere, for they say the Devil is a demanding master and his work is never done."

"That is a thing," said Peter, almost to himself. "That is a…" he shrugged as if in despair at not being able to express his awe at such a tale.

"I asked the vicar how far Lisbon was from here," said Zadok, "and he calculated from a compendium he had in his library that it was one thousand and seventy-seven miles as the crow – or the Devil – flies. It was indeed 'a Great Disturbance' as the journal worded it. Aye, a Great Disturbance, all right, that's what it was."

"So," said Wat Whysall, peering into his tankard and miserably cogitating whether he could eke out the dregs of his pint of ale for the rest of the night, "so, did y'ever go back down the mine again, Zadok?"

"No, I never did," Zadok said quietly. "I'd had my fill of that game, my fine lads!" He brooded a while, then said, "I'm old now, very old, and it's getting to be that I am surprised and grateful when I wake each morn that I am still here. I'm so old now that I forget things, but I shall never, ever, forget, long as I'm spared, standing down there in the Great Cucklett Mine. I told you they used to call it Never Fear Mine, and there's a grim joke for you, with me standing there in pitch darkness, crying like a child, with solid rock beneath my feet moving like water, while all the hordes of Hell galloped toward me, and their cannon boomed in the depths of the earth, and there was such a heap of groaning as if all the poor, afflicted souls, eternally damned to torment, gave voice in great number. I vowed never to go underground again, and my father got me an apprenticeship with the blacksmith here. 'Stick to horses, my lad,' the smith said to me. 'Lead could run out, or they find something better and cheaper, but man shall always need horses, and horses will always need shoeing! And so, friends, that is how The Great Disturbance took me out of the mine and made a smith of me!'

There was a long silence then around the fire, as each man thought of the story that Zadok had told. Some thought of the dangers they had faced and escaped, others of their own mortality, each man isolated by his inner reflections. It was a terrible thing they had just heard, and they needed time to digest it. The religious celebrants in Lisbon and those working Derbyshire men, each had been blissfully disregarding their own mortality, and suddenly Death gave a light cough of a reminder that echoed now in that dimly lit taproom. If the hand could reach out and touch thousands in one sudden strike like… so, why not this group around the fire, cosy and companionable of a winter's night? Or just one of them, each thought, in some way. It could be as they went home, or about their business or…why, even as they lay abed!

Peter stirred. He hated solemnity and had come to the inn tonight for merriment and good chaffing between companions, a happy night. It was sad, passing sad, the deaths of all those people, but the dead were dead, and life was for living. He needed a ruse, a segue into the rest of the night's good cheer he had planned when he stepped through the door of Tobias's premises. What better way than to play a joke, a ruse, on someone, but who?

He looked around the room, and his eyes lighted upon long-faced Wat, who by chance was sitting nearest to the window and through which he could see the snow-filled street beyond.

"Heyup!" Peter said, pretending surprise "Is that the vicar in his cassock, or old Ma Martin who's coming down wi' a jug for some ale?" At the same time, he winked broadly at the others, Wat being too busy peering into his tankard, gauging the few drops he had left.

Wat, who besides being a miser was incredibly nosy, rose and peered out of the window, and as he turned his skinny back, Peter rose and swooped upon the man's neglected pot on the table. He lifted it, and still grinning to the rest of the group, he poured the last few dregs of Wat's pot into his own and shook it over the floor to show it was now empty. He was not fast enough, however, for something warned Wat that it was a ruse. He turned while Peter was standing with both his own drinking vessel and Wat's in his hands.

"Hey!" Wat cried, "what game is this, young Thornton? 'Tis my pot in your hand there!"

"And so it is, Wat, my old friend," said Peter, "I er…, I er…" For once he was lost for words.

"You're never buying me a pint, are you?" Wat asked in mock disbelief, and this gave Peter his out, his cue to explain his action. He turned to the others and raised the tankards in his hands as if conducting an orchestra.

"In the spirit of comradeship and good company that is present here tonight, I intend to buy a round for us all. Drink up, lads, and let us thank Zadok for a wonderful story. Respect to you sir, and now let's make jolly, for you're a long time dead, say I!" he shouted out.

No one in the group needed any further urging, and swiftly the other four men drank up, and even Tobias and his grandfather drained their pots making eight pints the young joker had to pay for. It was too good an occasion to miss when someone got one over on Peter Thornton.

Tobias collected the men's pots and took them through to the barrels. Peter ruefully counted out his coppers to pay and Tobias laughed, for he had seen Wat Whysall give a broad wink also, to the other men. Wat had swiftly guessed what Peter's game had been, and Tobias whispered when Peter dropped the coins in his hand, "Upon my oath, but old Wat caught you there, my lad!"

"Aye," said Peter, recovering with a grin. "I know I've

been had! I had no other recourse, mark you, Toby, my friend. For all, we did not want another Great Disturbance here tonight!"

THE WITCH AND THE YOUNG WIFE

Once, and not so long ago neither, my dears, there was a farmer who had lost his wife, and had but the one son. One day, or it could have been in the evening, the old fellow said to his young un, "Look here, me lad, I'm getting on a bit now, tha' knows and..."

"Nay, father," said the young man, "You're still but a shaver!"

"Enough of thy chelp, my lad," said his father with a laugh, for they were very fond of each other. "Now, I'm thinking it's time to hand over the farm to you, but a farm this size needs a woman to help in the running, so look around, sharpish, and find yourself a good woman. When you marry, the farm's yours, and I'll help with it till you and your missus are running in harness as a pair. Got me?"

So the young fellow did as his dad said, and he kept a sharp eye out, but all the lasses in the village were either spoken for or dissolved into fits of laughter when he proposed. However, he got better at plighting his troth, and eventually, on a day trip to town, he found an absolute smasher, fell head over heels in love, and she thought he was quite fit, too, and things went well between them, and within a few months he popped the question and got a favourable answer. Whoop dee doodle, thought the young lad and took her home to meet his dad.

"Well," said Dad, when there was just him and his son together, and she'd caught the last bus or stagecoach or whatever home, "She's a very, very nice lass, and you two obviously go well together..."

"Like a pint of Ward's best bitter, a bag of cheese and onion crisps and a pickled egg," said the son dreamily. Truth to tell, he wasn't very romantic, but he was smitten, and so he thought of the things he loved best. He lacked the true romantic vocabulary. No Ploughman Poet, he. No Robbie Burns, that is.

On seeing his son's dreamy face, the old farmer snapped his fingers under his son's nose.

"Come back, son!" he commanded sternly.

"Oh, er, yes," the son said, and then recollected that his dad had some reservations about the girl he loved. So he asked him what they were.

"What are your reservations, Father?" he asked.

"Just the one," his father said, "She's a townie! They don't know our ways. They think different to us countryfolk. They think we are all hobbledehoys and don't know nothing."

Son rubbed his chin. "Grant you that," he said. "We shall just have to learn her right then, won't us?"

"Aye," said Father, "But I still don't know why you couldn't have picked a gel in the village. I allus thought you'd go for that Jane Boggs."

"What? Boggsy?" asked the son incredulously. "She's got terrible breath, and when she laughs, she neighs like a horse and then snorts like a pig when she breathes in, and she's got an enormous..."

"Turned you down, did she?" Father asked, who was definitely no shop egg.

"Nowt of sort," said Son, huffily. "Anyway, it's milking time. Goin' ter fetch em in."

Well, Son married the Townie, and after a week at Skeggie for their honeymoon, they came back to the farmhouse and the young woman set about learning the business of running a farm. The first thing she had to learn was milking, and she caught on very quickly, to father-in-law's surprised and approval. Next...

"Butter's a big thing wi' us," said the old farmer. "C'mon, I'll show yer how it's done."

He took her to the dairy next door, and, picking up a big pail of whole milk, put it in a butter churn, then again and again, till the churn was nigh full.

"Right, now this is what you do," said the old fellow. He put the lid on top of the old butter churn, inserting the churning stick and began to vigorously pump the whole swishy liquid, until it turned eventually from swishy to gloopy to sticky to delicious golden butter.

"Now this," said the farmer, scooping out the butter from the churn, "Is my best butter, we salt it and pat it to shape and wrap it, and ..."

"What do we do with this?" said the girl, looking into the churn at the liquid left behind.

"Why, that's the buttermilk," said the farmer and he gave her a cupful to drink, and she found it delicious.

"We sell that as well," said the old man. "It's good for building a body up, invalids, old folk, women having babies or nursing mothers. Or we mix it with taters and feed it ter pigs. Fattens em up no fuss. They loves it!"

"I see," the girl said, then broke off to hold her nose.

"Phew! What's that smell? It's like…" She sniffed again. "It's like snuff and cat-wee and wood smoke."

The farmer said, without turning round, "Morning, Aggie! And how are you, my dear?"

The girl looked round and saw in the doorway of the dairy, leaning on a bent wooden staff, a very old, very tiny… well, woman, she supposed. She was clad in flowing, ragged rags, broken shoes on twisted, swollen feet and a black conical hat with a bent-over top crammed over steely-grey, dirty locks of hair. Her face was a mass of wrinkles lined with dirt, and her big nose was a place where the warts all met. In her crooked,filthy hands she held a big jar with a lid.

"Come for me buttermilk," Aggie croaked, and hobbled forward. Waves of pungent odours wafted in with her, and the young wife hurriedly stepped back and covered the butter and open churn.

"Certainly, Aggie," said the farmer. "There you go, my dear." He scooped nearly half of the buttermilk into the old crone's jug, chattering all the while, almost as if he was wary of her, or… afraid. And as he spoke and hurried to meet Aggie's demand, three large black cats paced into the dairy slowly and sat around the old woman's crippled feet. They sat still as basilisks and stared unblinkingly at the farmer.

"Bless!" said the farmer, hurriedly finding three shallow bowls, and he poured almost the rest of the buttermilk into the bowls and put them on the floor. The cats paced forward as if linked and lapped delicately at the buttermilk. When they had finished, and the bowls were clean, they sat and licked their whiskers while the old woman fastened the lid on her jug and painfully turned around and hobbled to the door.

"Come, Paddock, Grimalkin, come, Harpier," she called, and the cats trotted after her.

"See you next week, my dear," called the farmer as the young woman fanned the air with her hand.

"Phwoar!" she said, "She stinks!" Then she realised that the old woman hadn't paid a bean for the buttermilk, nor had she even said thank you, goodbye or even kiss my fairy footsteps.

"Hey!" she said to her father-in-law, who was mopping his brow with one of those old, red-with-white-spotted hankies they used to carry. "Hey! The smelly old bat never paid!"

"Hush, child!" said the farmer. "They can hear you when they're far away! That was Aggie Withers, she lives up on the common, and we never charge her."

Humph, thought the girl, when I'm in charge of this dairy she will! And as for 'they' hearing at a distance, what could he mean? There was only one of old Aggie. Strange, passing strange, she thought. She put it from her mind, however, and concentrated on learning to salt the butter and pat it, and on the following day, she and Father took the butter to market and got a good price for it. A lot of folks asked for buttermilk, and the girl saw that she could fill the purse they carried even fuller if she sold that as well. Fancy little bottles, name of the farm on… Oh, she had plans!

So the following week when Aggie Withers fetched up at the door of the dairy, moggies in tow, she got short shrift from the new management. The new bride had started late and worked alone, but she was making a good job of it, and by her reckoning the butter – and what had formerly been Aggie's buttermilk – would not be long in the making.

"No buttermilk today," said the girl shortly. "Unless you want to buy some, that is?"

"Oh, so that's how it is, eh?" said Aggie, waves of effluvia washing off her and spreading into the room, causing the new dairymaid to blanch and gag. "Well, I'll not stop. I can see you won't have any butter this week, my dear. Come, my little ones!"

The cats did not follow but sat and stared at the woman for a while making grumbling noises, as if talking to each other, then they spat at her and stalked off.

Left alone again the woman wafted the smell away by fanning the door awhile, then returned to her labours. What did the old hag mean, she thought? No butter this week, why, it was well on its way to turning. She lifted the pole and twisted it, plunged it down, lift and twist and plunge, lift and twist and… but it was no good. For some reason the butter would not come, and she was left with a churn full of spoilt milk, which she eventually took to the pigsty and poured into the trough. But even the pigs would not drink it, backed away from the trough as if it held poison.

"How much butter did we get this week?" asked the son at the table that night.

"Errr, errr," said the young woman nervously.

"Did Aggie call today?" asked Father.

"Aye, and I sent her packing," said the daughter-in-law with some spirit.

"Did she say owt?" Father asked innocently.

"Said there'd be no butter," Daughter said. "How did she know?"

"Cos she's a flamin' witch," said the farmer, "And she put a hex on the butter churn. Did she say there'd be no butter ever, or just this week?"

"Just this week, and don't worry, I know what I have to do," the daughter replied. She hadn't believed in witches until now, but…

Sure enough, on the following Thursday, when the young woman started churning, the butter came thick and fast, and there seemed to be double the amount, which was strange, passing strange, and as much buttermilk again. And when Aggie and moggies arrived, their buttermilk was waiting. Aggie gave the girl a gap-toothed smile and said, "May the giving hand never falter, my dear. Don't worry; you look after me, and I'll look after you."

"Learns fast, don't she, Dad?" said the son that night, with a grin.

"Aye," said his father, patting his daughter-in-law affectionately on the shoulder. "Not bad for a townie!"

The following week, Aggie paused in the door as she was leaving and said to the girl, "You're with child, my dear. Eat well, don't smoke, or drink alcohol. It'll be a boy and it'll be ginger."

She did, she didn't, it was, and the mother called him Sandy as a pet name, and Dickon for posh. The other kids called him Ginga. Some things never change.

THE BUTCHER AND THE DEVIL

Many years ago there lived in Castleton a butcher called Nicholas Booth, a quiet man who was friendly with all his fellow men, but who spoke little and saw and heard much as a consequence. Though seemingly a very proper man in his dealings with all, he could not abide cheats, and would often turn the tables upon those who mistook him for a slow-witted man, He was one who kept his own counsel and acted when it best suited him, as this tale will tell.

Now, at one time, Nicholas had kept a butcher's shop and lived at Castleton, but later moved to Mottram, nearer to Manchester, which was then but a small town, King Cotton not having taken up residence there yet. He kept his contacts at the home of Blue John, Castleton, however, and would frequently walk to his old home and buy a flock of sheep and herd them back to Mottram, selling them off piecemeal to the other butchers of Newtown, Hyde and Gee Cross. He always asked a fair price and gave a good deal, often with a few pence returned in 'luck money', as the old traders called it, when a deal was struck, a custom still observed among some farmers in the Peak.

Often when Nicholas reached Mottram, the way being

tiring, he would stop to refresh himself at a pub there called the Bull's Head and take a pot or two of ale. The landlord and his wife were a sharp pair and were up to a few tricks they played upon their customers to increase their takings. It did not escape Nicholas's attention that the pots were just that bit smaller, the ale that little bit weaker, than in other pubs and inns he frequented. Nor were the supposedly pint pots always filled to the top. Old George and Joan were adept at doing this, as they were at short-changing drunks. The dishonest pair had never met or even heard of Max Thursday, but they would have agreed with his epigram, 'Scruples never earn money.' As an honest man, it irked Nicholas Booth to see such a dishonest practise go unchecked, and he quietly resolved to himself to serve them right when the occasion arose. In the meantime, he kept his own counsel and bided his time, as do most Castleton folk.

The chance came one dark and dirty night, midst rain, thunder and lightning, Nicholas arrived back in Mottram from one of his trips to the Peak, tired and footsore, but content. Of a goodly flock of sheep that he had left Castleton with early that morning, he had but one left, and that a large black tup, a ram, with eyes as yellow as candle flames glowing in the dark, a pair of massive, curling horns, and a fleece black as the Devil's own. Maybe it was this that put the idea into Nicholas's head, and he called to mind then how ready George and Joan always were to protest their respectability by calling on the lord to judge them, the devil to take their enemies, and, being terrible gossips and slanderers, how quick they were to judge others and call down the wrath and judgement of Old Nick upon those they reviled.

"Devil take the man for serving me wrong," George

would say of some imagined slight he had suffered.

"May the good Lord send a dark angel to torment them…" Joan, a miserable little wretch, would say.

They were very inventive in their vows and imprecations, and believed in the forces of darkness so strongly that Nicholas muttered to himself as he took hold on one of the tup's horns, "This just might work, it just might…"

Pulling and pushing the old tup, who was tired and cranky from the long walk, the butcher persuaded the creature to go with him to the rear of the inn, and when he looked through a side window as he struggled past, he saw that both George and Joan were in the taproom, seated at a table with company which meant, since they were too mean to keep a servant, that the rear of the premises would be clear for him to enter and stage his little deception.

Nicholas opened the back door as silently as possible, lifting up on the latch after he had sprung it, so that the door didn't catch on the floor and make a noise. Rolling thunder and the odd crack of lightning covered any small sound he might make. He pulled the ram into a passageway by one horn and drove it before him until he reached a side room which served as a cellar or stillroom, containing the barrels, set on cold stone thralls. The ram trotted in placidly, and Nicholas caught sight of a bucket of slops, stale beer that miserly George would put back in a lively barrel of mild, as was his practise.

"Just the jolly job, my lad!" breathed Nicholas to the ram, "Here, cut the dust and wet thy whistle!" and he placed the bucket in front of the tired and cross old tup, who needed no second bidding. Nicholas left the animal getting a good three pints or so of strong, flat ale down its neck and crept out and back round to the front door of the inn. That'll ginger him up, thought Nicholas as he walked into the taproom of the Bull's Head, or 'The Napper' as it was known locally, a 'napper' being another name for a head, whether human or animal.

In the dark depths of a gloomy room sat George and his miserable spouse Joan, keeping company and drinking by the light of a cheap candle with Stephen Fullalove, the parish clerk, and Tinker, the sexton. Nicholas shook the rain from his coat and seated himself on a low stool at their table, Nicholas exchanged greetings then told them his 'news', news so fresh that it had only just been made up as it left Nicholas's lips.

"Have y'heard about the devil escaping at Castleton,?" he asked the somber quartet.

"No," said Tinker, "What's to do, Nicholas?"

"Well, you've heard of that big cave they have there, called The Devil's Arse?" he asked.

"Aye," said Stephen. "They reckon it goes down further than can be measured. Down to Hell itself."

"That's the one," said Nicholas. "Well, they started digging for Blue John or lead or summat down there and they kept chucking the rubble down a deep 'ole, and all of a sudden there was a flame shot up, and a growling and shrieking, and more flames come out, and a whole legion of demons came flying up, led by the Devil himself, and now they are roaming the country causing all sort of mischief!"

"God be with us!" shrieked Joan. "We shall all be killed in our beds!"

"Aye, well," said Nicholas. "The trouble's dying down back there, but those escaped evil demons have spread into the countryside, and I reckon summat followed me back here tonight. I could hear it scampering behind me and shuffling and rustling its wings behind the walls along the way, in between cracks of thunder!"

"Oh, merciful heaven! Saints preserve us!" quavered George.

"I said me prayers, I can tell you," Nicholas said, nigh choking with the laughter which he held back. "Another mile or so, and I reckon it would have got me! Joan, could I prevail on you to pour me a pint of your best ale, me dear, for I am needing it sorely!"

Joan got up and lit a guttering candle from the other one on their table and went into the corridor, heading for the stillroom. Nicholas kept his face turned away from the others, pretending to warm his hands at the meagre fire by the table. He waited eagerly to hear the landlady's scream when she caught sight of those great, yellow, slitted eyes glaring back at her in the candlelight. There came no sound, but she was back in a trice, her hand that held the candlestick shaking wildly and the other held over her heart as if she was about to suffer a seizure. She was whey-faced and trembling like an aspen leaf.

"Oh, George, my love," she quavered, "Go and fetch a jug of ale from the still-room, for there's something in there that I don't like the look of! Its eyes shine yellow and it grunts and huffs at me, and it smells like the devil himself! I fear Nicholas has brought the evil one to our house!"

With much grumbling George rose unwillingly to his feet and stumped angrily down the passage. He was back in less time than his wife, however, with his mouth working and his eyes rolling madly.

"Stephen!" he shouted to the parish clerk, "If there's a devil in this world, he's in our cellar now!"

The clerk rushed to the passageway and there beheld in

the dim light from the cellar the shadow of a large beast with monstrous horns. Suddenly the light was blacked out as the creature moved in front of the candle and Stephen clapped his hand to his mouth in horror as he saw two evil yellow eyes staring madly at him, unblinking, and then the dim light was restored as the thing before him moved, and he saw a bulky, four-legged beast approaching slowly and with purpose. It stopped and shook its wicked horns from side to side; lightning flickered through the windows and lent the snorting ram an unearthly glow.

It was too much for Stephen. He yelled to George that he was off to fetch the expert in these matters – the vicar – as he bolted out of the inn's front door. Tinker the sexton took a peek down the passageway, and he followed the clerk, wisely, though treacherously slamming the inn door to as he left, imprisoning those left behind. He did not wait to give a reason as to why it would take two people to bring one vicar but disappeared into the thunderstorm outside.

Nicholas Booth said nothing, nor did he make a move to help, hugging himself to keep from laughing out loud at old George and Joan, who were too afraid to tackle the devil in the passage, but too miserly to leave their inn unguarded. While George held the passage door firmly closed by leaning on it, he muttered fervent prayers under his breath and his wife wailed and bemoaned their fate. Finally, when she could find no one else to blame, she turned on her husband.

"How many times have I told you what'd become of us if you kept using those short-measure pots?" she screamed. "And watering the ale and spirits down? What did I say?"

Nicholas Booth shook his head sorrowfully but was too magnanimous to pronounce judgement upon the pair. Meanwhile a drunken tup bumped on the door with its bony head and curling horns, making the pair jump.

"It was the Excise you were afraid of!" George hissed, "Not, not..." he indicated the door, which was shaking under the impact of a solid skull and a pair of lethal horns.

"If I ever get out of this with my soul intact, I'll smash every one of those pots, as God is my witness," George panted, pushing against the bulging door and gagging on the stench of stale beer and peat-wet, unclipped wool that wafted through the gap.

"I'll never short-change a drunk again," Joan sobbed, forgetting that Nicholas was listening to their confessions.

A few minutes later Stephen Fullalove the clerk and Tinker the sexton returned, ushering the vicar in before them. He was a tall, thin young man who looked as if he'd taken more services than nourishing meals, but though he was pallid in countenance, he seemed determined and had come equipped to exorcise the demon or fully-fledged devil, for he held before him a small handbell such as is used at Mass, a large church candle which he lit from the low fire, and the book, the Holy Bible, all a good man needs to quell and exorcise the forces of evil. He hoped. He hoped, but his faith was being sorely tried. Meanwhile, the ram had grown tired of butting the door, and having worked up a thirst it had retreated, back down the passageway to finish the bucket of ale in the cellar and look for another way out.

Ringing his bell, reciting a prayer, and holding up his candle, which cast about as much light as the parsimonious publicans' weak tallow had earlier, the vicar advanced, with everyone but Nicholas following cautiously behind him. Entering the stillroom, he saw the 'devil', who had drunk another two or three pints and was now both well 'blootered' as the Scots say, and extremely cross with the world in general, as it had become wedged between two barrels. Holding the candle even higher the vicar called upon all the powers invested in him, all the strength of the established church, all the power of the Almighty, whatever else he could call to mind, and he resolved that if the evil being from Hell approached one step further, he would give it a sweft at the back of its horns with the large church candle which he carried in his trembling hands. Direct action and muscular Christianity might prevail where all else failed.

Seeing so many folk all coming at once in some sort of procession towards him, the black tup took fright as well. He wriggled free from between the two barrels, and one crashed to the floor behind him, lending the startled intruder wings. He bolted towards the equally frightened humans before him, giving out a mighty, belching bleat as he came, which was probably partly due to the beer imbibed. A moorland ram rarely drinks alcohol, certainly not to excess, as this one had. All it wanted was a nice field in which to sleep it off.

Head lowered, back legs pumping and sliding on the stone-flagged floor, the drunken, terrified tup caught the clergyman a hefty clout above the knees with his wicked horns before the vicar had time to sweft him with the large candle, and the cleric fell backwards, knocking over George, who also fell backwards into Tinker, who fell too. In falling, Tinker knocked Fullalove the clerk, who knocked over the miserable old Joan, until the whole passage was a sea of waving arms and legs, and a din of screaming and swearing and praying for salvation which, along with the thunder, which sounded as if it was directly overhead, fortunately, drowned out Nicholas's bellows of laughter. With a final, unearthly bleat the ram made an almighty leap, and with one bound he was free, clearing the writhing, moaning, yelling bundle of humanity in the narrow passage. He skidded into the taproom and in passing gave a sideways glare at Nicholas, the instigator of all this shemozzle, then the ram imitated a blacksmith and made a bolt for the door. The dark night beckoned beyond, and the belligerent boozy brute disappeared into it. Nicholas drained his pot and followed. His work there was done.

Although they had foresworn their cheating ways, in the weeks that followed George and Joan found the straight and narrow hard to cling to. It was, to them, as the ancient sage once remarked, 'as the sapling bends, so grows the tree.' Deep stuff. But basically they found that they could not go straight. However, tempted as they might have been, they remembered that they had confessed all in front of Nicholas Booth and could not go back to their crooked old ways either. No longer able to make the tavern pay, since they had driven away a lot of their custom, they put it up for sale.

Now, there's an opportunity, thought a certain Mottram butcher, and within a month or two, 'The Napper' had a new, and very popular, landlord. People who had stayed away from the Bull's Head when the miserable pair ran it, came to the tavern. The beer was good, the pints were indeed full pints, and the change was always right. Nicholas Booth thrived and was a happy man.

And the tup? Well, history is a funny old thing, and the trouble is, all this happened a long time ago, and since it involved no one famous, no one really paid it much mind, or thought about setting it down for the record. So, you pays your money and you takes your choice, but there's two main stories as to what happened to him.

The first is that the old black tup ran straight back to Castleton and took refuge in The Devil's Arse, or what was regarded as a fairly accurate representation in stone of his Satanic Majesty's fundamental orifice. Not having seen both yet, we can't help in any comparison. But if you ever do go – to Castleton, that is – and happen to venture into the aforementioned cavern, look out for a pair of yellow eyes, glowing in the dark.

The second story, and the one I choose to believe, is that Nicholas Booth went in search of the tup and brought him home, and the animal spent the rest of his days in a nice grassy meadow behind The Napper, and grew very, very partial to a bucket of beer slops brought to him daily by the landlord, and if anyone ever asked why he kept the ram in such luxury, Nicholas would pull on the tup's horns affectionately or comb its lugs with his fingers and say, "Devil knows, I owe it all to this old lad!"

SMILER AND THE HARD STONE

Once there was a silly man who worked as a roadman on the roads around the Peak. That is to say, he broke big stones up into small stones and he filled in the holes in the road with them, so that the carts and carriages and coaches had an easier, less bumpy passage on their travels. He had a variety of tools: a little hammer, a big hammer, and a 'tumper' to bash the stones down into the holes and make the surface smoother, and a wheelbarrow to carry his tools along the road and to take the stones he broke to the holes he filled. He was very fond of his work and enjoyed the physical labour of breaking stones to the required sizes.

One day he found a really big stone lying in the grass at the side of the road. He thought to himself, "That's right size for that 'ole over there, once I've broke it up into smaller bits!" So he hit it in the middle with his small hammer, which was quite a heavy one and took some strength to lift and swing, but the stone didn't even budge. So, he swung his hammer really hard and fetched it a mighty bash, but it still had no effect. It wasn't even marked by the impact of the hammer.

"Right, lad," said the silly man to the stone. "I'll sort you out!" And he took his coat and waistcoat off, for he had worked up quite a sweat already, and he pulled his shirt sleeves up, showing his bulging muscles which he had built up from all his years of stone-breaking, and he hitched his trousers up and tightened his belt.

"It's Smiler for thee!" he said, addressing the stone sternly, and he went to his wheelbarrow and fetched his friend, Smiler, out of the barrow.

Now Smiler wasn't what you or I would call a friend, but the silly man looked upon Smiler as one. Smiler was a great, big, huge, enormous sledgehammer, which most people couldn't lift, let alone swing like a toy above their heads, as the silly man could. With Smiler and the silly man, no stone was left uncracked.

Usually, that is.

The silly man took up a stance, his legs akimbo and firmly planted, Smiler's head resting just against the edge of the rock, and the silly man firmly gripped the ashwood shaft and, raising Smiler high above his head, he brought him down with an enormous whack.

There wasn't a mark upon the stone, but Smiler vibrated in the silly man's hands and stung them, so that they tingled and smarted. The silly man dropped Smiler, put his hands under his armpits and danced around the roadway in his hobnail boots for a while, which was a sight to see. Fortunately, there was no one to see the sight, for which the silly man was grateful, for he took it as a slight that he had been bested by a simple rock.

"Well," said the silly man, bending over the rock and panting, "You may think you've won the contest, but I've got a trick up my sleeve, my lad! I'll learn thee!"

And the silly man picked up the big rock with some

effort, staggered over to the wall at the side of the road, and threw the rock into a field.

"There!" shouted the silly man. "That's taught thee a lesson. Just lie there! And think on!"

CROOKER

Anyone with a sensitive enough nature, anyone who has a 'feel' for those other worlds which live alongside our world – and which quite often stray into ours, sometimes even taking up residence here and living with or off us – anyone with that gift, I say (some say 'curse'), knows that there are places best avoided, particularly at night. These places are usually quiet, neglected spots, where a person hurries by, not knowing why they do so. Some things live and brood in these places which mean no good to man, and though one is safe by day, or unreachable when racing by in the warm security of a motor car, by night, on foot, a traveller goes in peril of their life and, some say, their very soul. Scoff if you like. I merely tell the tale.

Such a place that I speak of can be found along the road which runs from Lea to Cromford in Derbyshire, alongside the swift and often dangerous River Derwent. In some places the road runs close to the rushing waters, so close that one false step can send the unwary benighted traveller tumbling down the bankside and into the river. At other places the road veers away, as if frightened of what might lurk in the watery depths, waiting for what darkness and ill fortune might bring it. This is the haunt of Crooker. He seems to have been there for centuries at least, for he is spoken of in old, old stories and all these stories agree. They say that though he is in our world, he is not of it. They say he is large, shapeless, or shape-changing, and hunts mortals by moonlight. Some have spoken of a large black creature being seen to cross the road in a flowing motion, while others say he has been known to stand upright on the very edge of the banks of the Derwent, among the alder trees, so still and black that he could be mistaken for one. Until it is too late for the unsuspecting traveller. He has a maw and a voice, a terrible voice, and that is about all that is known, for anyone who knew him better did not live to tell the tale.

So dangerous a route to travel was the relatively short Cromford to Lea road that in medieval times a small chapel was built by Cromford Bridge. There, travellers might light a candle at the small altar and say a prayer to the saints to intercede on their behalf and protect them on their way. If you walk into Cromford Meadows and look, you will see the ruins of that chapel still.

A story that has come down to us through the ages concerns a young man, a traveller, who was hastening one late winter's afternoon to Cromford, where his mother lay ill. Word had reached him of her condition, and he had set off directly, for he was a dutiful son. As he passed through Lea, he saw that night was coming down fast, and he shivered to himself, for he had heard when he lived in Cromford, of Crooker and his ways. A man called to him from an inn to put up there the night.

"It is dark now, look," the man cried, "And the moon will rise soon. Do not travel that way, young master, if you value your very life and soul!"

The young man shook his head and walked on. Sure enough, over a hillside nearby sailed a full, white moon,

Cromford Bridge, where the Crooker lurked

which seemed to stare down mercilessly upon him and show him up on the black, dark road in silhouette a morsel for such as Crooker.

It was then that he saw, coming down the hill from the direction of Tansley, an old, old woman, all dressed in green gown and hat, the colour of a witch. She hailed the young traveller and asked him, "Where whither, young man? Why travel you on such a lonely dangerous road so late in the even and under a baleful moon?"

"I'm for Cromford. My mother lies ill, good dame," the lad answered.

The old witch shook her head.

"Not on this road, nor yet by this moon, or it shall be that your life is forfeit," she said.

But the young man was steadfast. Sighing, the witch gave a cry and reached up into the dark sky above her pointed hat, and a large raven flew down and settled on her shoulder. It held something in its beak, reached its head down and placed it in the witch's withered old hand. She hobbled forward, leaning heavily on her crooked staff and placed in the lad's hand a bunch of Saint John's Wort, freshly picked and in flower, though it was the depths of winter and all was bleak and sere upon the ground.

"Here, take this," said the witch. "You saved a bird from a net once. That bird was my friend. Hold fast to it, for it may save your life this night. Give it to Crooker when you meet him. But give the other gifts you receive first."

"What other gifts? Who is Crooker?" asked the young man, but the witch had gone. Gripping the St, John's Wort, a powerful charm against evil, he journeyed on and the darkness grew about him. He had not gone more than a few steps when there was a rustling in the hedge and another old woman walked out and stood before him. She wore a cloak which was green like the gown and hat of the first witch.

"You should not travel the road to Cromford by night, when the moon is full," she warned him.

"I must," the traveller replied. "My mother is ill, and I must be by her side."

"You are a dutiful son," the old witch said. "What is more, you saved a hare from a cruel snare once, and she was my friend. Here, take this." She brought out from under her cloak a posy of primroses, which shone palely in the darkness.

"Give these to Crooker when you need to," she said. "They will help you. But remember to give the St John's Wort last of all. The Goddess be with you this night." She vanished into the darkness as the traveller called to her and asked what kind of man Crooker might be.

"You fool!" a voice called before him. "Crooker is no son of man! Turn back and be saved."

He groped his way forward and found a third witch waiting for him, wrapped up warmly in her green cloak.

"I cannot go back," the traveller said. "Have you a gift to help me?"

"Yes, I have," the third witch said, reaching beneath her cloak. "Here, for the sake of the fox and cub you saved from the huntsman's trap. You have a good heart, boy, and in saving my friends you have earned my help this night. This is my gift to you." She handed the traveller a bunch of daisies, still freshly blooming, although frost was in the air.

"Keep far from the Derwent," the old witch called back as she headed up the hill toward Riber. "Do not leave the road for anyone or anything, and make sure you are on Cromford Bridge before the moon is risen."

The traveller hastened on, clutching his magical gifts, but it was hard travelling in the darkness, thick as the Devil's nutting bag. Each step he took he tested with his foot outstretched and trembling, expecting any moment a slip or fall into the river at his left shoulder, seeming nearer to him every step, with its sinister gurgling and plashing over the rocks, calling him to a gasping watery death. All the while the river seemed to be chuckling nastily at his elbow, as if to say, "We'll know each other better ere long, my friend!"

Close to Cromford bridge the road bent into a curve to the left, and as the traveller took a step forward, the moon came out from behind a cloud and flooded the lane with twisted, tormented shadows from the huge alder trees which towered above him, dancing, swaying shadows seeming to leap towards him, surrounding and clutching at him. From out of the shadows, heaving itself up onto the river's bank, came Crooker, black as the depths of Hell, twisted and warped and ever changing its shape like a giant leech of evil, and as it limped towards the traveller the river screamed out, "Hungry! Hungry! Hungry! Give to me, Crooker! Give to me!"

"Here, Crooker! Take these," shouted the traveller, and hurled the posy of primroses at it. There came a loud splash from the river and the malevolent shadow shrank back. The traveller jumped to the side of the path nearest from the river and ran for the bridge, his heart in his mouth.

Again the foul shadow rose high above him, its gnarled fingers grabbing for the man, and the river Derwent, white-flecked and fast-running, yelled out, "Hungry! Hungry! Give me, Crooker! Give me!" The traveller took the posy of daisies and hurled it at figure of Crooker which was rising again on the path ahead, writhing in a sickening dance before him. As the daisies hit their target Crooker spat and hissed in alarm and pain and shrank back. There came a splash from the river and the traveller made a few more yards headway before the foul twisted being blocked his way again.

"Hungry! Hungry!" Give me, Crooker!" the river wailed in anger as the traveller sidestepped Crooker and got one foot upon the bridge. Crooker lunged forward and wrapped its evil black shape all around the young man.

The traveller did not need to take aim. He turned in Crooker's embrace of death and thrust the bunch of St. John's Wort straight into the heart of the dark, foul being which enveloped him.

There came a startled, spitting sound like a fire being doused, and the traveller felt himself picked up like a feather, spun around a few times, then thrown out of the grip of Crooker and onto the safety of Cromford Bridge, whilst a keening sound as of a thousand tortured souls in torment rose up into the air and was torn away by a fierce wind. The river sobbed and sank back in its bed, and the traveller crawled on his hands and knees over the bridge to the Cromford side, to the old chapel of refuge, towards the door, then the sanctuary of the altar, too weak, too frightened to rise to his feet.

The villagers in Cromford had heard the screaming in the night and bolted their doors firmly. With daylight, they came down as they had before, to drag some poor wretch from the river's clutches, they thought. Instead they found the traveller, still on his knees, at the chapel's small altar. The villagers helped him to his feet and took him outside. There they showed him where an enormous and aged alder tree had been ripped from the bank of the river and hurled across the road, its dead and rotten branches like huge, grasping fingers torn and splintered where it had fallen.

Some say that tree was Crooker, and the power is long gone. Others, who know the old ways, think that he still lurks beyond the edge of darkness, waiting... waiting... They will not tell you this for fear of being scoffed at. But they never travel that stretch of road after darkness has fallen.

THE 'FISH-GHOST' OF OLD BRADWELL

I just had to include this story for readers who like the surreal. I include it because it is remarkable to me in that I have never heard of a ghost which has been transformed. Exorcised, or banished, yes, but… Anyway, I shall spoil it if I talk more on it, so here it is:

Bradwell, or Bradda, as it is more fondly known, is a strange village, and one that is of great antiquity. It has been occupied at least since the invading Romans came for the lead deposits, so plentiful in the area, and there was a belief that the old population of Bradwell was descended from'Phoenician slaves, brought there to mine the lead.

Whether the occupancy of such a small dale by so many souls for so many centuries leaves traces of ghostly mien is debatable, but a likely explanation, for the fact remains that Bradwell seems to have more reported ghosts to the square foot than any other Peakland village, and a researcher will find some very strange and unsettling tales of supernatural appearances in and around old Bradda.

The strangest story of what appears to have been a haunting has to be that attached to a house in the quaint old area of Hill Head in the village, the house being called somewhat unimaginatively Hill's Head House. At a time in the 1700's or even a little earlier, it was believed that there had been a murder of a child in the house, most reports having it that a young girl was the victim. The corpse had been buried under the staircase but, denied a proper Christian burial, its spirit would not rest. At first the spectre was content to appear every night at the foot of the stairs, near its long-concealed grave, but it began to be seen elsewhere in the vicinity until many people in the area were so frightened that it was determined that help was needed to 'lay' the ghost, and the advice and assistance of John the Master was sought.

John, whose surname is hinted at in an old book as H__th_e, was a master of occult arts, but strangely also a member of a baptist christian sect, which worshipped in the village. He was a master of astrology, herbalism and was also supposed to be a necromancer, that is, one who could reanimate and converse with the dead. In the village he was regarded with both respect and fear, and none doubted his capabilities, for he had often given proof of his mastery of these arts. After some discussion, John agreed to lay the ghost.

The wise man came to the haunted house at an appointed time to find that a goodly crowd of villagers had assembled outside the house, and more than just a favoured few were crammed into the room in which the ghost would manifest itself. It is said that John brought the necessary tools for the work in hand, but it isn't recorded exactly what he had, save for a humble stick of chalk, with which item he drew a circle in the middle of the floor, while the onlookers were bid stay against the walls of the room. It was time to raise the ghost and then, having bound it with a spell, to exorcise it. This, by the by, shows that John considered himself to be a magician, not a witch or warlock. A magician works inside a defined circle, into which any malevolent spirits cannot enter to cause harm; a witch works outside a circle and raises the power she uses inside the circle before directing it to her specified use.

Inside the protection of his magic circle, John knelt and prayed, and commenced an incantation with such fervour that his face literally ran with sweat. Suddenly, the onlookers were to say later, they felt the floor move mightily, some reporting that it bucked up and down for several yards in a fast, rippling motion. John rose to his feet and in lowered tones said, "Berald, Beroald, Balbin, gab, bagar, agaba!" which is supposed to mean, "Arise! Arise! I charge and command you!" and the spirit appeared. No record exists, unfortunately, of what shape this spirit took, whether it was the likeness of the murdered child or not, but it must have caused quite a stir in that small room packed with onlookers. John then said to the ghost, "In the name of the Father, Son, and Holy Ghost, why troublest thou me?" That is all we have of the ritual, and we do not know if it appeared to sight, but having established mastery over the spirit, and safe inside his unbroken, charmed circle, John bid the spirit to depart in the shape of a fish, and henceforth to locate itself in the Lumb Mouth, which was the outlet for an underground stream which sprang from the rock. On Christmas Day, it was enforced upon the bound spirit that it would take the form of a bird, a white ousel, and fly a distance of two miles or so to Lumbly (or Lumley) Pool and there take the body of a fish again. Master John then dismissed the spirit and bid it to return no more. From then on, the ghost walked no more in Hill's Head House.

It was said for many years after that on Christmas Day

when people went to draw water at the wells by the pool they saw the fish, and tradition held that they would run away, shouting in fear, "The fish! The fish!" As late as the early 1900's this story was still known in Bradwell, and one writer remembered how the story preyed on his mind when young, and he recalled how he used to crouch down and run in fear past Lumbly Pool if he was out in the dark and had to pass that way to get home.

What I find strange about this story is that everyone writing about the events presents it as a 'ghost' story, when it is quite clearly something else. Admittedly the account, first published in 1862, around a hundred years after it was supposed to have taken place, mentions that the spirit is supposedly one of a young child who was murdered and buried beneath the stairs of Hill's Head House, but the original account says – and all writers after this repeat the fact – that the people of Bradwell, while ever the story was told, always referred to the spirit which Master John raised and bound as being a boggart.

And a boggart is a very different thing from a ghost.

A ghost is the earth-bound spirit of a human being, sometimes of an animal, as in the galloping horses which are heard but never seen on dark nights at Dethick crossroads, above Matlock. The spirit of the ghost is held captive, it is believed, as a result of some transgression in life, or because of great grief, love for the site, a violent death, and so on. However, a boggart is not held captive. It is a 'genius loci', which was believed by the Romans to be the geographically defined protective spirit of a place. The boggart is found in folk stories all over the British Isles, and its name gave origin to the word 'bogeyman' or 'bogey', also 'bugbear' among others, though the first two have been taken to mean ghosts.

There were believed to be two kinds of boggarts. One was the household boggart, which played nasty tricks on the inhabitants of the house, such as souring the milk, causing butter not to churn, causing loud noises at night with no discernible site of origin, and causing household animals such as dogs or cats to go lame. A boggart would also crawl into a sleeper's bed and place a cold, clammy hand on the person's face. They could be kept at bay by fixing a horseshoe over a house doorway and leaving a pile of salt outside a bedroom door. The second and more dangerous kind of boggart inhabited lonely places and had a liking for marshes or holes in the ground, and would try to lead travellers astray at night, often drowning them if possible. Children were believed to be abducted by a boggart if caught alone at night on a dark road or walking through lonely places.

In Derbyshire the boggart was usually claimed to be a big black dog the size of a calf, with a shaggy coat and glowing eyes as large as saucers. The Gurda Boggart patrols the road between Wensley and Winster and is still encountered occasionally. A young woman walking that way some years ago claimed to have been followed all the way by 'something' which she described as having just a face! There was another boggart on the road from Matlock to Snitterton, and a boggart, shape unknown, hid in a hole near Birchover at Shale Hillock, a hole which ran deep into the roadside wall and into a bankside. Passers-by would occasionally hear it gurgle at them, which must have been quite unnerving in the dark.

Boggarts are also sometimes described as being shapeshifters and can take on any form they wish to, an important point in the case of the boggart of Hill's Head House.

Now, bear in mind that the ghost at Hill's Head House was supposed to be that of a young girl. There is no record or explanatory tale attached to the old accounts of this story to any murder of a child in Bradwell, and surely if such a thing had occurred, the murderer would have been caught and punished or at least tried for the crime, leaving some sort of record, so it can be assumed that the story of an infanticide in the house was a myth. Could a boggart have picked up on the anecdote and taken on the form of a supposed murdered child to torment the residents of the house? Living cheek by jowl with the humans in the house it must have been privy to all their doings, lurking in the shadows, listening and watching, as boggarts do. As it gained strength or daring, it took its 'haunting' outside the house and was seen in the lanes and alleys of the area. House Boggarts don't seem to have been tied to the exact purlieu of their residence, otherwise there would be no point putting a horseshoe over an external doorway! Perhaps whatever house boggarts there were had been there before the house was built, and thus resented the human inhabitants as interlopers, which would give us a reason for their malevolent behaviour.

If we take the spirit in the house to have been such a malevolent boggart, then what Master John did was the 'binding' of a spirit. When a ghost is exorcised, it is generally 'sent on' to a better place, released from its bonds. If it is not a ghost being 'laid' as it is called, it can be a demon, which is 'raised' during the exorcism, then generally banished and sent back to its master in Hell. A boggart, or genus loci is an entirely different matter, for it has, it seems, always lived on Earth. It is no wonder Master John prayed long and hard, for he had to first 'raise' the boggart, 'bind' it, order it to assume a different shape, that of a bird, then assign it to a new location, where it would take the form of a fish. Quite a day's or evening's work, and it is no wonder that he perspired freely.

The words quoted as having been used by Master John in summoning the spirit to come before him are interesting too: 'Berald, Beroald, Balbin, gab bagor agaba!'. It isn't known what language – if any – these words are from, but they occur in several old grimoires, magicians' workbooks, and are the words used in Necromantic rites. It seems strange that whoever passed this story down to William Wood and assured him that it all happened a century or so before, could remember the words so accurately. What I feel happened is that when Wood came to writing this story down in 1862, he had access to a treatise on black magic. Several grimoires as they are called, although originally handwritten, were in print in the 1800's, having been in circulation since the middle ages, though claiming to have greater antiquity even than that, including the Key of Solomon, supposedly written by the wise king himself. In several of those grimoires this spell or invocation is quoted and is specifically used for the purpose of raising the dead and causing them to speak to the magician. Since this is not what Master John had in mind when setting about the exorcism, I suspect Wood threw these exotic occult words in to add colour to his tale. We have no way of knowing now. It all happened a long time ago, in a crowded little room in Bradwell, and all we have is the fragment of a fascinating story.

A BAG OF NUTS

Once there were two young men from Calver, rogues both, who cared little for honest work and stole from their neighbours under cover of darkness. In that manner they supported themselves.

One evening as it was growing dusk, the two thieves set out for nearby Baslow, where one of them intended to steal a sheep from the meadows by the river. When they reached Baslow churchyard one of the young wastrels concealed himself in the church porch to listen for anyone approaching from the village, and his friend carried on down to the meadows to steal the sheep. While the man in the porch waited he began to crack and eat a bag of hazel nuts he had brought with him.

Now, the sexton of Baslow, who was a very superstitious and highly-strung sort of fellow, had as part of his duties to ring the curfew bell each night. The bell was rung to alert people working in distant fields and to guide them home to keep them from being 'benighted'. Those bells have saved many a labourer or traveller upon the highways in the Peak. As the sexton came to ring his bell he walked through the churchyard, mumbling his prayers, with his mind dwelling not on his appeals for divine support, but on the malevolent beings who are supposed to haunt sites where the dead are buried.

Hidden from view in the concealing darkness of the porch sat the young man who was supposed to be on watch for such as the sexton. He cracked the hedgenuts with his strong young teeth, munching happily, wishing only for a pint of beer to wash the nuts down with. They were a little dry without a drink, he thought.

The sound brought the sexton to a swift halt, and for a while he stood in silence, peering into the blackness of the church porch, trying to see who – or what – was there, whilst his superstitious mind ran riot. Seeing nothing, he invented the worst to fill the vacuum of supposition, as do most people.

"Tis the Devil himself!" he moaned, "He's sitting in there devouring wayward souls. Heaven knows there are many who have fallen from grace in this parish!"

It was then that his own guilty conscience assailed him. His nerve broke and he turned and took to his heels as fast as his flowing cassock would allow. He'd go and tell the parson, he decided. He'd implore him with his superior authority to go and drive the Devil out of the church porch and back to the infernal regions over which he reigned.

Now, the parson was not cut from the same cloth as the sexton. He was a stout and jolly man, fond of the pleasures of this world. He was so fond indeed that he suffered from gout and sat with his bandaged foot upon a stool in his parlour when the sexton called and was shown in by the parson's wife. When he heard the sexton's tale he dismissed it with a laugh, saying, "Go and ring the bell, you fool!" but the sexton would not go alone, and begged the parson to accompany him.

The parson was plainly faced with a problem, for if he did not go the bell would not be rung, yet he could not walk to the church, for his gout was so painful that he could manage but a few steps. In vain he cajoled and pleaded with the sexton, but the poor man was clearly in a very frightened state and would not go alone. When all the parson's wheedling and bullying had failed the parson appealed to the sexton's better nature.

"Come, man," he wheedled. "You see how I am. On my word as a Christian and vicar of this parish, if I could get there without walking, I would come with you!"

Got him there, he thought. Time for my evening glass of port. Or two.

The sexton was not without a certain skill in guile, either, and he came up with a solution.

"Why, then, I'll carry you, reverend," he said, smiling triumphantly. "I'll give you a piggy-back, down the garden path and in through the side-gate."

Got him there, he thought. Dash, thought the vicar. He has me there!

And so, puffing and panting and staggering and lurching, the sexton set off down the garden path with a rotund cleric on his back, the gouty leg stuck out like a hoopla peg. Slowly and painfully the sexton carried the vicar, he going slowly, the vicar finding it painful with each jolt, and so, panting and groaning, they approached the dark porch where the thief was hiding.

As they came close to the porch the moon broke through dark obscuring clouds and the thief, peering out from the porch where he sat, saw a man approaching, bent over under the weight of an obviously heavy load. Thinking it was his larcenous friend approaching with a stolen sheep, he called out eagerly, "That looks like a fat 'un. I'm famished!"

This thoroughly unnerved the sexton, who feared his

time had come, and deciding to sacrifice the parson, he threw him to the muddy ground, shouting, "Aye, and you can have him if you like!" He did not look round to see if the Devil did indeed devour the parson, but made full pelt for his cottage, clearing the church wall in one bound, nor did he stop running until he had reached his own door, which he shouldered open, gasping for breath, and barricaded it against any pursuer. He did not venture out until the morning light. Unschooled as he was in the ways of the world, he did not know that there is more evil, more cunning devils, walking abroad in the daylight hours.

Lying in the mud where he had been cast, deserted by his sexton, and with what he thought was the Devil approaching him, the parson forgot his gout, and with fear lending him wings, he ran nearly as fast as the sexton had to his own home, where he locked the doors and prayed all night for deliverance from the evil which had visited his parish.

Shortly after the sexton and parson had fled the second thief returned with a fine fat sheep, and the two neer-do-wells, having done Satan's work for him that night, made their way back to Calver, leaving only a few scattered nut shells on the floor of the church porch for the shamefaced sexton to discover in the morning. He swept them up quickly and did not bother telling the parson.

THE LITTLE RED MAN, OR: THE GINGER FELLER

Twice upon a couple of times... Well, it was once upon a time, but I get fed up with writing that. I mean it's every story in this genre that starts that way, innit? Oh, well... better press on.

Once upon a time in a little village called Wensley, in the Peak District – not Wensley in Yorkshire where they make the cheese, but Derbyshire where... well, they don't make much at all there nowadays. Used to be leadmining and farming, I suppose, but now there's just a bit of farming and that's about it, really. Anyroad up, where was I? Oh, yeah, right...

Well, there was this farmer, see, and his wife. Don't know their names. I suppose I could ask around, but I don't live that way anymore. It'd mean a long bus trip and once I got there I don't suppose anyone'd remember 'em. That's how it goes, you know. Folks don't socialise like they used to. They've got their cars and their big tellies and cheap ale from the supermarket and... okay, okay, I hear you.

Well, this couple, the farmer and his wife, that is, they had three sons and their names (which I do know) all began with a 'J'. Don't ask me why. Some mums and dads are weird that way. There was Joe, who was a nasty piece o'work, Jay, a right tightwad who wasn't much better than Joe, and not very bright either, and Jack, who was all right, a decent skin, as the Irish say. For Wensley, that is.

Anyway, the old feller and his missus lived a very quiet life in their little cottage. They had a cow for milk, a sheep for wool, a hen for eggs and a bit of a field for vegetables and such, but not much more. And the lads got tired of having not much more, so one day Joe, the eldest, decided to see if he couldn't find something a little better than bread and scrape every day, with an egg thrown in now and then. I've no idea why his parents threw eggs at him. I'm just telling you the story as I heard it, more or less. Let's crack on, as Joe's dad said when he threw the egg at him. Terrible yolk.

"I'm off," said Joe, at the door one day. "I go to find my fortune, ta-ra, all."

"Door!" shouted his mum, who was a bit nesh, and there was a heck of a wind blowing over Masson Hill from Bonsall way (Bonser, G'bless yer, as they used to say). "Dunner forget yer snap. It's on the side," she bellowed.

So off went Joe, with his packed lunch (snap) in his pocket, determined to seek fame and fortune, come what may. I'll head towards Buxton, he thought. It's all happening there, I hear.

He walked on for several miles until he was on the High Road near Parsley Hay, and there he saw a large flat boulder under some trees at the roadside, and he sat down to eat his snap. While he was eating, he heard a voice coming from the trees.

"Is that cheese you've got there?" asked the voice. "And home-made bread wi' real butter? Good show! Gizza piece, mate!"

Joe looked over his shoulder and saw a little man all

covered with red hair (well, it gets right cold up there, round Parsley Hay, I can tell you!). He was about the height of nine pennorth of copper coins, which is about three pence decimal, and he stood there, licking his chops and rubbing his tum-tum.

Now, as I've said, Joe wasn't a nice person. He was permanently dissatisfied and always looking to quarrel with someone, and even worse when he'd had a drink. He looked, as his grandma used to say, as if he'd seen his bottom (though she didn't say bottom) in a mirror (well, he couldn't have missed it, for it was a big one!) and didn't like the look of it, and to be honest, his face wasn't much better. He was a sour young individual, all right.

"Gerrout on it!" said Joe and gave the little ginger man a kick on the leg, and the poor little ginner limped off, back into the woods.

Joe got up and went on, and by the time he reached Parsley Hay it had started to rain, and as he reached Harpur Hill turnoff it became curtain rods. He was hungry and beginning to agree with Oscar Wilde that ambition is the last refuge of the failure.

"I'm none a failure," he told himself. "I'm off home for me tea!"

So off he went, giving a sour look at the wood at Parsley Hay as he passed, to see if he could get another kick in at the little red man and cheer himself up a bit, but he was nowhere to be seen.

Joe settled into home life again, but Jay, who wasn't very bright as I say, decided that he could do better than Joe and he determined to head off to Buxton and beyond to seek his fortune. He got his mum to make him a big sarnie, and she wrapped it in greaseproof and put it in his pocket, and he put his coat on and she helped him with the buttons cos he wasn't really very good with complicated things, and off he set.

"See yer all later!" he shouted.

"Put 'wood in th' 'ole!" screamed his dad, who was as nesh as Mum, and mardy as well, and that wind was blowing something chronic over Masson Hill.

Off Jay went, with a smile on his gormless gob, hoping to find sovereigns growing by the wayside. But the further he went, the more dispirited he got, and hungry too, so he sat down on a big rock at the side of the road, close by Parsley Hay, under some trees, and got tucked into his mousetrap (cheese to you) buttie.

"I say!" came a voice. "Have you got fresh bread and some spiffy cheese, comrade. I'm so hungry my tummy thinks my throat's been cut! Spare a morsel, do!"

Jay looked and saw a little red man, still not tall enough to make a shilling in loose change, all covered in hair, and coming his way, still limping from the kick he had received some time before.

"You just wait there," said Jay, and he slowly and deliberately ate the sandwich while the little ginger geezer watched with shining eyes, licking his lips.

Now Jay was notoriously tight. He never gave anything away, and even looked both ways before breathing out. There were moths in his wallet that had never seen daylight, and the heads on his coins blinked when he brought them out to count them, so he was hardly going to treat the little fellow to some of his snap. He stood up when he had finished and brushed the crumbs off his jacket onto the roadway.

"Help yersen," he said cruelly, "And dunner stint!" It will come as no surprise to you, I am sure, when I inform you as

I do now that lack of interpersonal skills, the development of which was sadly neglected in his early youth, meant that Jay had few friends in his limited social sphere. A morose, misanthropic and miserly youth, he was strictly Billy No Mates down the pub, and was only ever invited to family functions, where the drink was free and where he would try and hit on the female guests with terribly corny patter which he thought 'smooth'. We've all met the type, as now had the hairy ginger man.

The little fellow found a crumb and a tiny sliver of cheese amongst the grass and gravel of the roadside.

"Well, it wasn't much, but the thought was there – sort of," said the little red man. "So, I'll give you a tip. Go in the woods and look for the mine that is there. You might find your fortune if you've eyes to see, and the gumption to make something of it."

Well, Jay went into the wood, but all he could see was a tumbledown old hut with a mineshaft in the middle of the floor, over which hung a rickety-looking windlass with a big bucket attached to a rope wound round the barrel of the winding gear.

"Why, it's a worked-out old lead mine," he said. "I'm not going to waste my time with that!" Like I said, no gumption. I mean, if some magicky-looking tiny being gives you a tip, you take it. Bear that in mind. But poor old Jay's heart just wasn't into this fortune-seeking, and besides, he was getting hungry again, and missed his mum. Those old apron strings, eh? Stronger than the drag chains on the Queen Mary.

"I'm off home to see what's for tea," he thought. "All this ambition's made me hungry!" And off he went, and his mum was glad to see him, and it was macaroni cheese. His favourite.

A year or so went by and things were still bad at home, and the youngest lad, Jimbo, had grown up enough to be heartily sick of his loafing brothers, so he said, "That's it! I'm off."

"I thought it were wind blowing this way from Enthoven's factory," said Dad, who was a master of wit and repartee, sniffing theatrically. "Whither thou, pray?"

"I'll pack you some snap, lad," said Mum, and off he went.

Sure enough, when Jimbo got close to Parsley Hay, he came to a wood on a bankside by the road, and he sat down on the big boulder, which hadn't been moved, to take his refreshment. A big doorstop of homemade bread and cheese, avec pickled onions, and a bottle of cold tea. Good adventuring grub. He gripped the butty, and was about to bite into it, when the little red hairy man popped up from behind the large stone.

"That's never bread and cheese is it?" enquired the little red man. "I'm starving! Chuck us a piece, me duck!"

Jimbo was a star. He hutched up on the rock and patted the space he'd made.

"Sit yersen down, ginner," he said, "And ay some er this!" And he tore the sandwich in half and offered it to the little chap, telling him that there was some good cold Yorkshire Tea to wash it down with.

"Nay, nay, lad," laughed the red man. "I was but testing you, to see if you are worthy of the quest I will point you to. Finish thy meal, and then I will show you something that will make your fortune, if your heart is as stout as it is kind."

Ooh, don't he talk funny, thought young Jimbo. Perhaps he's from Ashbourne. So, all excited about the quest he'd been promised he wolfed down the sarnie and necked the tea, and wiping his lips told his companion he was ready.

The little man took him through the wood and pointed to the hut, then held the door open. "A fortune awaits you!" he told Jimbo with a wave of the hand towards the bucket.

Well, Jimbo thought long and hard, then he thought, nothing venture, nothing gain. What have I to lose? Your life, came back the answer from somewhere deep inside him, but then he thought, shurrup. This is an adventure. Here we go! So, he got into the bucket, and the little red man wound Jimbo down the shaft of the leadmine.

Now, Jimbo wasn't as brave as he cracked on to be. He closed his eyes and held onto the rope for dear life. Eventually there was a bump! and he opened his eyes and saw that he was in a beautiful country, with green fields, and waving trees of fragrant blossom and clear, limpid streams flowing through. This is a bit of all right he thought, then there came a little cough at his side.

The little red man was at his elbow – he had slid down the rope and was waiting with a suit of armour, complete with helmet and visor, and a bright, pointy sword and a shiny shield.

"Here, lad," little Red said urgently. "Whack these on you. There's no time to waste!"

"Hold on," said Jimbo, "You didn't say this might turn violent!" But he might as well have been talking to thin air, for in no time the little red fellow had Jimbo all suited up and lethally equipped.

"Just look at the quality of this suit and, ahem… accoutrements," said the strange little man, sounding like a salesman boosting his product. "Sheffield's finest stainless steel. Look at the shine on your shield!"

"Errr…, what's to do?" asked Jimbo, struggling into the armour and hefting up his sword and very shiny shield.

"Well, there's a princess or two, damsels in distress..."

"I thought there might be," Jimbo said grimly, half thinking to himself that he was dreaming and that he'd wake up any time at the side of the road. "It's all a bit improbable, this, you know..."

The little hirsute being interrupted Jimbo. "There's no time for this," he said urgently. "There's a princess in a copper castle and she's being kept prisoner by a copper giant. His name is Copernicus. You must kill the giant and free her!"

"Shouldn't we just tell the coppers and leave it to them?" Jimbo asked, but his reluctance – and his weak joke – was lost on his audience. The little sprite snapped his fingers and produced out of nowhere a small copper ball. He threw it down on the floor; the ball spun, emitted a few sparks and a humming sound, then rolled off swiftly.

"Follow the ball!" the strange being shouted. "Follow the ball, Jimbo! Make your fortune!"

Well, Jim got quite excited, and off he went after the ball, though he found the going hard, dressed in a glorified tin can and carrying a heavy sword and shield. Soon he came to a valley where all the grass and the trees and the little birdies tweeting in them were copper-coloured, and there in the middle of the valley was a gleaming copper castle, surrounded by a moat of molten copper. The copper drawbridge creaked down, and the ball rolled up against the copper door of the castle, banging repeatedly upon it.

"Oi! Copper knickers!" the ball shouted (because of course it was a magic ball so it could speak), somewhat insultingly. "Come out here and fight, you big heap o'metal!"

There came a big clumping and creaking noise, and over the drawbridge walked ponderously with huge steps a copper giant with copper armour, a copper shield and a copper sword. Coppa load of that, thought Jimbo.

Jimbo didn't quite know what to do at first, but the giant did. He swept his great copper sword round his head, then aimed at Jimbo's juff, and if Jimbo hadn't ducked, he'd have been a few inches shorter and a lot more dead. The giant staggered a bit with missing his target, and Jimbo thought to himself in a flash, why he's top-heavy! All that copper up top and he can't balance right, just like me dad when he comes home from the Red Lion or the Crown Inn. So, he took a whack at the copper giant's knees with his sword. There was an almighty clang! then a bit of a rumble, then a lot of one, and then the copper giant just fell to bits in front of Jimbo and the little red fellow.

Jimbo was ecstatic. He danced wildly round, best as he could in his suit of armour, then he grabbed the little red man's arms and danced round with him till they were both out of breath.

"We did it! We did it, Ginge!" shouted Jimbo. "Er, I mean, matey." Some folks can be a bit touchy about their hair colour, especially when it covers their entire body. So he said hurriedly, "No offence."

"None taken," said the little ginger chappie. "What are you doing?"

Jimbo was gathering up all the copper into a heap, and a tidy pile the giant would make, he was thinking greedily.

"I reckon I've made a start on my fortune," said Jimbo. "There's a lot of good clean copper scrap here. I'll drag it back up to top of th' 'ole, an' get a wagon to take it back with me. There's a feller out at Tansley does scrap. I reckon he'll pay me a fair few bob..."

"Stop!" shouted the little man, and he danced again, but this time with impatience. "You've not done yet!"

"What's to do?" asked Jimbo.

"Well," said the little red man exasperatedly, "I know you're from Wensley, but even they must know the rules applying to fairy tales."

Jimbo scratched his head, then a smile broke over his face.

"A damson in a dress!" he cried. "You can't fool me!"

The little sprite sighed. "Damsel in distress! Sometimes," he said, "Sometimes… Come on!" and he pushed and tugged Jimbo over the copper drawbridge and up into a copper tower, and there they saw a copper-studded door with a big copper padlock. Jimbo gave it one mighty hack with his broadsword and the lock flew off. The little man opened the door gingerly, since he was a redhead. Jimbo just groaned at the bad joke.

Inside the room was a beautiful young maiden, combing her copper-red tresses and sniffling a bit.

"What ails thee, maid?" asked Jimbo, getting into the spirit of the story.

The young woman leapt to her feet and ran towards Jimbo and his companion. Eyup, thought Jimbo, we're right here. But it was not to be. When the maiden reached her noble saviour, she lifted his visor and peered inside the suit, gazing long and hard upon his visage. That is, she took a squiz at his chops.

"No, I don't think so," she said firmly to the little red chap. "I mean, I know the rules of this game and all, but I really don't think that 'happy ever after' could come out of any relationship we might enter into. He does nowt for me, sorry. 'Sides which, I make it a Tuesday. Mum always does mince and tatties for tea and I'm fair starving," and off she skipped, down the stairs and off up the copper trail, back to her wee home in the north where tatties and mince is regarded as being somewhat of a delicacy.

"That's it, then," said Jimbo, somewhat downcast. "I'll just take this off and go home myself. I'll be back with a wagon for the scrap tomorrow."

The little red hairy man laughed scornfully. "Not so fast," he said. "There's more to this, old lad." And he clicked his fingers again, and pulled out of the air a silver ball, which shone in the sunlight. He threw it down onto the ground and it whirled around a few times, threw out a few sparks, then rolled off at a fair rate, over hill and down dale.

"Hi-ho, Silver, and awayyyyyy… Gosh, this is such fun!" shouted the red man, laughing madly. Clanking away behind him in his suit of armour, Jack was out of puff and lost for words.

Eventually the ball came to rest at the top of a hill and waited for Jimbo to catch up. Once there, he saw below him a valley of waving, silver grass and silver trees in which sang silver birds, and there, surrounded by a silver moat was a large and beautiful silver castle.

"Let me guess," said Jimbo. "Inside that castle…"

"Same as before, only this time think silver," said his escort. "Off you go, and if you'll take my advice, use a reaping motion with your sword. Anything above grass, lad."

The ball rolled down the silver hill and over the silver drawbridge and knocked loudly on the silver door to the silver castle.

"Oi! Long John Silver!" it shouted, "Get your sad and sorry silver-plated botty down here, pronto! Sir Jimbo of Wensley would joust with thee!"

"Silver-plated?" came an outraged bellow from an upstairs turret, "I'll have you know there's a hallmark on my..."

Fortunately for those of a sensitive disposition, the rest of the protest was drowned out by a heavy clumping noise, as out onto the green, no, silver, sward charged a ginormous giant made entirely of silver, whirling around his head a huge club made of the same metal, which glinted in the sunlight. Whish! it went as it almost parted Jimbo's hair through his helmet. Jimbo ducked and made with his sword as if he was scything Long Meadow back home. He connected with the silver ogre's ankles and sliced them through as effortlessly as the Co-Op bacon slicer when he fetched his mam's order for the week. The ensuing crash of a heap of silver higher than Solomon's Temple in Buxton (when it was built some centuries later) was deafening.

"Now for the damson in a dress," said Jimbo who still believed in true love despite his earlier disappointment, and he clankily climbed the spiral silver staircase in his heavy armour up to the imprisoned maiden.

Imagine his surprise when he reached her room to find it unlocked and the occupant, a rather fetching young lady in a silver gown, packing a suitcase.

"You fool!" she snarled at Jimbo. "We were getting on so well! I'd got the big lunk just where I wanted him! Another week and we'd have been married!"

"You mean…?" asked the little red man, hooking a thumb through the window at a big, glinting heap of scrap silver. "You? And him? You? Him? You and him?"

"And why not?" snarled the little silver-digger. "He was years old and well overweight. He couldn't have lasted much longer. He'd have been worth a fortune when I had him cremated!" And she grabbed her suitcase, ran downstairs and, pausing only to snatch up the giant's silver leg, she dragged it off behind her up the silver road to mum and home.

"Come on!" the little man urged. "No time to waste!" He pushed and shoved the bewildered knight errant back downstairs and off down the dale while Jimbo was still trying to estimate how many wagons he'd need to cart off his latest heap of booty.

Reaching the top of the next hill, the little red stirrer clicked his fingers and manifested another ball. This time it was a golden ball, and it fell to the grass where it spun pure... pure... well, gold in the sunlight. Jimbo's avaricious eyes nearly fell out of his head, and he pulled his visor down and began to prepare for the next jaunt. Off whirled the golden ball with Jimbo and the wee guy in pursuit, leaping streams and vaulting walls and dodging round grazing sheep.

"Eeh!" panted Jimbo to his miniscule matey, "It's just like one of those platform games they haven't invented yet, innit, Ginga?"

"Super Mario?" asked Short Stuff.

"Yeah."

"Never heard of it. Come on, we're falling behind!"

At the top of the next hill the golden ball stopped and waited for them to catch up, whirring and whistling impatiently. Jimbo reached the top of the hill and whistled too. Below him in a golden valley with golden grass and... well, think copper and silver castles and surrounds, as were earlier, change it to gold and you've got this one. Pure, butter-yellow twenty-four carat gold. Jimbo's mouth watered and he thought, this is it! Crack this and your fortune's made. Then he thought, my luck can't hold for ever, what if...

"Errr... any handy hints on this one?" he asked his hairy colleague.

The vertically-challenged man stroked his furry red chin.

"Nope," he admitted, then, cheerfully, as he stepped

back to watch the oncoming fray, "I'm sure you'll think of something. Son, you are on your own!"

"Heard that somewhere before," Jimbo said bitterly, and trudged off toward the golden castle.

Over the drawbridge and up to the golden portcullis raced the golden ball, coming to a halt and bellowing, "Oi! Goldilocks! Down here now! Sir Jimbalot of Wensley and Winster is going to make a scrapheap out of you!"

"Errr…, it's just Wensley, actually," whispered Jimbo, having a fondness for Wensley and a dislike of the neighbouring Winster ever since the Girda Boggart had chased him home one night.

"Has to be Winster, or the joke won't work. You'll see," the red man said out of the corner of his mouth. He was a great one for surprises, was old Ginger. He skipped backwards, with a "See you later, I hope!" and was gone.

"Oooh, Mum!" Jimbo said, and his stainless steel knee-pieces knocked together noisily. "Any ideas, Ball?"

But the ball had gone. Truly, Sir Jimbalot was on his own. And from inside the castle came a great roaring and rampaging. It grew louder and louder as doors opened and slammed to again, and over the drawbridge came the biggest of the three giants, so tall that rooks were nesting in his hair. Golden ones, of course. Nothing cheap about your man.

"Sir Jimbalot of Wensley and Winster?" the big fellow shouted in a golden voice that shook the welkin (search me). "More like Sir Winalot, and Wednesday, a Ginster's, for I'll make dog meat of him today, and midweek a Ginster's meat pie if there's anything left!"

"No," said the little red man, from behind a sheltering hillock, "Doesn't really work, that gag. We may have to cut that one out."

Jimbo said nothing. He couldn't; his teeth were chattering too much. He looked at the giant then he reflected on his own miserable size in comparison and tried to see what advantage he had. He couldn't see one. It was alright thinking of David and Goliath, but with that great big golden, sweating.... Sweating? Yes, the giant was sweating in the hot afternoon sunshine made even hotter by being reflected off the golden grass and the golden castle, and as he wiped his brow, a glittering cascade of molten gold fell onto the ground and made little teardrops of solid precious metal at Jimbo's feet.

Jimbo stuck his tongue out at the giant, with his visor up, and made certain gestures which are considered unacceptable in polite company, then turned and ran away, round the castle moat.

"Catch me if you can, y'big heap of brass!" he yelled.

Well, the giant wasn't having that. He was twenty-four carat pure gold, and then some, so he huffed and puffed and chased Jimbo round the castle. Suddenly, when the sun was behind the giant, Jimbo stopped and aimed his best Sheffield stainless steel shiny shield (try saying that with your teeth out after a few pints of Wards) full in Golden Boy's face. The concentrated beams of sunlight blasted rays of heat straight into his fizzog, and, gasp, wonders of wonders, the giant's whole head began to melt! It was not a pretty sight. Barrels of sweat fell and cooled into pieces no longer as big as teardrops, but these were the size and shape of duck eggs. Solid lumps began to fall off the brute, a whole ear nearly brained Jimbo, a great big golden tongue fell with a thump and waggled in the grass like a crocodile, an eyeball... well, you get the picture (which is more than the eyeball did!). The whole golden structure slowly dissolved before Jimbo's gaze, and he was left standing alone with a pile of riches beyond the dreams of Ava Rice.

"Well done, well done, Champ!" said the little red man, coming out from his safe spot, and reaching up to pat Jimbo's back. Back of his knees. "Now for the damsel!"

In the furthest, highest turret, Jimbo smashed the lock off a solid gold door and found inside, spinning golden thread on a golden spinning wheel, a beautiful maiden with hair the colour of yes, (ahead of me, are you not?) a raven's wing (sorry to disappoint you). She looked up and said, "My hero! My knight in... well, it got soppy after that, but suffice it to say, she was well taken with Jimbo, and he with her. Can't wait to show her to me mam, he thought, and he took her hand and led her downstairs until they came to where the little red man waited for them both.

"Help yourself to the gold," said the little chap magnanimously and Jimbo picked up a few choice pieces. The giant's sweaty duck eggs filled Jimbo's pockets and the hood of his George top, and he hoisted a still-intact giant's arm up and threw it over his shoulder.

"I'll come back with a wagon for the rest," he said.

"Errr... 'fraid not," said little Red. "The whole lot, copper, silver, gold, goes back to normal by dusk and it's getting late now. The mine shaft will close over and I will regain my kingdom, which is all the land you have seen, and a thumping lot more beside. Didn't I do well? Whatever you can carry, and the love of a fair young damsel, is my kind reward to you for your trifling service." The cheek of it!

So, Jimbo refilled his pockets and picked a bigger length of giant-gold, and the damsel blushingly admitted that she was wearing beneath her maidenly gown bloomers with very, very strong elastic at the knees and waist, and they got quite a bit in those, because she was a big lass. They bid farewell to the little red man and climbed back up the mineshaft with some difficulty, considering the weight they were carrying in scrap gold, and Jimbo took his fortune and his lady back home with him to Wensley. His mum and dad were so pleased to see him, but his brothers got rather bitter and twisted about it all, and said, well, they would find something a lot better than a bit of scrap and a bird with big knickers, which just goes to show where their chauvinistic heads were.

Jimbo married his golden lady, and with their fortune they built a modest palace over toward Brightgate, and he bought his mum and dad a bungalow in Darley Dale, and they all lived happily ever after, apart from Joe and Jay, the worthless brothers, who spent the rest of their lives scratching up little holes all around the area. And if you don't believe me, you can still see some of the holes in the fields around Wensley and Winster where they dug. Don't fall in. The little red man has gone.

THE MERMAID OF THE BLACK MERE

(Blakemere Pond, sometimes called Black Mere Lake, is a small natural lake which lies between Buxton and Leek, six miles north-west of the latter. Legends have it that there is a mermaid in the pool, some saying that she is malevolent, others that she can grant immortality to the person who sees her. The pond is supposed to be bottomless, and inexhaustible.)

A still summer's night with hardly a breath of wind. Bone white, a full moon shone down upon the man who trudged alone, heading up the rough moorland path towards Black Mere Pool. It was a night for travel, and the young man took it gratefully. He couldn't stay down there, in his room, where the walls closed in and he saw again the sights, smelled the stench, was there again with all the horrors that he had witnessed…

He was a broken man, a man who had seen too much, a young man grown old before his time, a man who had walked into a living nightmare which had changed him for ever. So now, at nights when the memories were strong and he could find no rest, or when sleep did come and the nightmares followed readily and he was transported back there in his dreams, he walked. And walked.

He'd come to live here after the little village near Buxton had become too much for him, and soon he would have to up sticks again and walk on to somewhere new, always heading north, following the backbone of England, the Pennines. Try as he might to keep his distance in the places where he settled, the people of the place grew used to him and with familiarity came attempts at friendliness, and though he wanted – sometimes desperately human company, after what he had seen he could not make small talk any more, could not return the easy word, the homely badinage that other people tried to draw him into. He lived daily with his memories and had seen what people did to each other.

Somewhere in the valley below an owl called, to be answered by another nearer to him, but he paid it no mind, and when he came to the large pond, the Black Mere, he sank to the ground and lay on one side, resting his head on a cupped hand, looking out over the water, the soft turf his bed for the night. He had crushed with his body the wild thyme which grew amongst the wiry moorland grass he lay upon, and the sweet fragrance mixed with the honeyed aroma of heather in bloom.

How long he lay he didn't know, but the night deepened, and the moon rolled round till it laid a path across the water, and he suddenly saw the surface of the little lake part, and a pair of white, slender hands, pressed together as if in prayer, glide towards him, a small wake of water breaking behind them. At the same time, he heard a sad, wailing note that rose and fell like the waves that broke on the bank's edge near him. He watched impassively, not starting, or even blinking. The waves parted, and a pair of arms broke the water, then the head and shoulders of a beautiful young woman appeared a few yards from him and gazed upon him.

Her long silvery hair fell about her shoulders, the skin of which seemed to possess a greenish tinge in the moonlight, and it was clear when she stood that she was as naked as a fish.

"Do I not frighten you, mortal?" she asked, in a voice that sounded like small silver bells chiming, and she arched her long, graceful back, then leant forward in a sinuous move like a snake about to strike, over the edge of the pool, to look closely at the young man, gazing directly into his eyes.

'No,' he said simply, "You are a dream, that is all. My mind is not what it was before I went for a soldier, and I imagine many things. That is all you are, either a sleeping dream or a waking one."

"Then what of this?" the nymph of the waves asked. She flipped effortlessly over, and long, shapely legs appeared where her head had been, and she had gone, swimming back under water away from him.

All was silent for a minute or more, then some distance away across the small lake, but clear in the moonlight, the waters burst open in a huge spout, and from it a horrendous hag surfaced, clad in filthy-looking tattered rags and ran across the surface of the water, on skinny legs. She was but a rag and a bone and hank of hair, as the poet had it; her broken, jagged teeth clacked fearsomely as she cackled at the sight of the young fellow, her eyes flashed red above a crooked, warty nose, and her bony arms were extended, hands with dirty black talons reaching out to snatch up the young man.

Yet he did not flinch, and at the last minute the apparition halted, filthy talons still outspread, became a mist that turned to pattering droplets of water which fell back to the surface of the mere, and in its place the young water sprite was back at the water's edge with her chin resting on her hands, looking up slightly at the young man.

"That's never failed before," she confided. "Most men would run screaming into the night, back to their little world of light and warmth. Why not you?"

Propped on one elbow, almost at a level with the nymph's green eyes, the young man attempted to shrug.

"I've seen death and horror," he said simply. "I've seen things far, far worse than that. My mind has not been... not been well, and the things that I have seen come to me in my sleep nowadays. They come often. When I can sleep, that is. That is what is happening now. I have fallen asleep here, here on this bed of grass and thyme. You are just a dream, and soon I will wake up and know that's all that you were." The girl nodded, then pushed herself backwards from the bank and, cupping her hands, she unexpectedly threw a goodly amount of ice-cold moorland water in the man's face. He sat up abruptly, sputtering and wiping his face with his sleeve.

"Awake now?" she enquired in a tone of mock sweetness. "See me still, or am I gone?"

"I see you," he said slowly, then to himself, "Am I truly losing my mind? Am I mad? What are you if I haven't lost my reason?"

"I," said the young woman grandly, "am the mermaid of Black Mere." She spread her arms before her and mock-bowed gracefully.

I will humour this apparition for a while, thought the young man, and he asked, "A mermaid, truly? This far from the sea? How can that be?"

"Well," she said, "the villagers below think that I came here for love of a mortal. We are supposed to have fallen for each other and he smuggled me back to his home in the valley below. I'm supposed to have met and fallen in love with a young sailor, the way mermaids do, I'm told. He lived down there, below the moor, in the village called Thorncliff, and such was our love for each other that he visited me every night. When he died, I was heartbroken…"

Here the maid clasped her hands over her heart in a melodramatic posture and the moon lit up her beautiful figure, her rippling, cascading hair of golden yellow, so that the man caught his breath in wonder.

"Heartbroken," she resumed, "and my love turned to bitterness, and I began to lure travellers to the lake and drown them. What think you of that tale, traveller?"

"Well," he said slowly, staring at the beautiful young woman before him. "I suppose you could be a mermaid…"

"Pah!" she exclaimed, did a perfect backflip, her legs reaching up to the sky, then back under the dark surface of the water.

"Did you see a mermaid's tail?" she enquired sweetly, swimming back to him, lissom as an eel.

"No, I…" He was lost for words, caught under her spell.

"As for the sailor bringing me here, why I knew Thorncliff before it was called such, even before it was named Thorntileg, the clearing in the thorn trees. I have been here since the waters formed."

There was a rustle in the heather and a fox appeared at the water's edge, took a drink, and was gone.

"See," the maiden said. "The creatures do not shun me, or this place. The villagers say this lake is cursed, which is why it is called the Black Mere. They say that no bird will fly over, nor beast drink from it. A man used to come here – such a fool – and bring others and tell them the tales of this place. He used to recite a doggerel poem. Would you care to hear it?"

"I would," said the man, and she stared solemnly into his eyes and recited in mock sepulchral tones:

"A lake that with prophetic noise doth roar;
Where beasts can ne'er be made to venture o'er—
By hounds, or men, or fleeter death pursued,
They'll not plunge in, but shun the hated flood."

The maid laughed and said, "One day, as the man was leaving after telling all his lies about me, I gave him the scare of his life upon this earth! I showed myself to him in the guise of the hag, and he fainted clear away!" She laughed merrily. "They had to carry him back down off the moor, and he never came again!" She mused on this for a while, picked some duck weed off her shoulder and flicked it playfully at the reclining soldier.

"Of course, other men say that I am here because of a man named Joshua Linnet," she said, musing with her head on her splayed fingers which rested on the bank's edge. "What children men are! How vain! Everything has to be of their doing!"

"What did he do, this Joshua fellow?" her companion asked. He shivered, and pulled his jacket tighter. As the night deepened it was growing colder, though the naked water sprite seemed not to feel it.

"Well," she said, "I am supposed to have been once a beautiful young mortal maid, and I spurned a village lout called Joshua Linnet. For revenge he named me as a witch, and the villagers believed him and brought me here, bound me and threw me in the water. As I sank below the surface and drowned (though witches, I'm told, are supposed to float!) I am believed to have cursed young Linnett, and three days later – ah, three! A magical number in your world! – master Joshua was found floating in the pool, his face clawed to ribbons by the Witch of the Lake, the one you did not flinch from! So… young traveller, which do you think I am? Mermaid or witch? Siren or vile sorceress?'

"I don't think you are either,' he said slowly. 'I don't know what you are. You are not a dream, nor mermaid, nor witch. What are you?"

"Hmm…" she mused as if to herself. "Should I tell you? Perhaps, but first there must be an exchange. Something from you. Tell me how you came to be here, man-creature!"

He stared away, down into the valley, then looked up at the stars, diamond-bright and cruelly cold, impassive. He looked away from her and cleared his throat.

"There's been a war out there," he said simply, waving his hand at the world below them. "They sent for me, and I went, and I think I was a good soldier. I was in the thick of the fighting, always. I saw things that would turn most men's stomachs back home, but I fought on, sure that we had right on our side. And we won. Towards the end of the war… Towards the end…" He broke off and plucked at the grass distractedly. She took one hand and laid it upon his. It was cold, icy cold, but he felt comfort in the touch.

"Towards the end of the war," he resumed, "We were getting closer to the enemy border, they were surrendering as we pressed them back and we came… We came to a camp. A big one, a prison camp, with wire and guard turrets and prisoners in striped uniforms, men and women, children, even. Those that were still alive – and there were many dead – were like skeletons, their eyes huge in their heads. The sights, the stench. I shall never, ever get it out of my mind. The men who guarded them were soldiers, smartly dressed, well fed. They came out of the camp and saluted us, offered their surrender as if they had fought honourably..."

"They wore uniforms? They were soldiers?" the maid asked, then, "Hush! I will look!" She stood, hip deep in the shallows, threw her long hair back, and drew one hand over the surface of the waters before her. She blew gently and muttered strange words, and the water became like a dark glass into which she peered.

"I see them," she said, "They bore the crooked cross on their armbands, a death's head was on every man's cap, and they wore double-lightning flashes on their collars. They considered themselves the cream of their army and their actions just. Ahh! What evil lurks in the hearts of men! What did you do?"

"The man who opened the gate for us after the surrender kicked a prisoner out of the way. The poor creature was so weak he fell and lay in the filth, too weak to rise. I shot the guard dead and would have shot more if my own men had not taken my pistol from me. They sent me to a field hospital, and then home, and I was in a .... in a place for quite a while. Then one day I found they could not keep me, so I just walked out of there, and I walked and walked, and every time that people get too close to me, or the dreams become too strong, I walk on. Eventually, I hope, I shall find somewhere where I can feel safe and whole again. And that is my story." He stopped talking and stared impassively before him.

"Do you have no one, mortal?" the maid asked gently.

He looked at her and shrugged. "No one who cares. My parents died years ago. I have a sister somewhere, but I don't know where. I've met many like me, tramping our roads, family gone, home gone…"

"And did you gain nothing from this war of men?"

"Yes, I did," he said savagely. "I learned never, ever, to trust men again! I learned that if you give people a uniform, or a badge or a flag and tell them that this is theirs because they are special, that others are their enemy and mean them harm, there isn't much in the shape of cruelty that they won't countenance once they have swallowed the lies. They'll torture and murder and…"

"Hush, hush," she said and reached out and laid one cool, graceful finger on his lips. "You are safe for a while. You are in my world."

"Who are you?" he asked.

"Well," she said, laughing a little, "I am not a mermaid. I am a maid of the mere. Do you see how the muddleheads confused me? Mere maid? Mermaid! And so, I have become a story that is told to frighten children, one that is preserved because it is thought quaint, though once I was more, much more, than a tale told to children. I am a spirit of the water and without me man would soon die. I was a nature goddess and the people of old worshipped me, brought flowers and other offerings on special days to me. Now I am just a silly tale, and one day that too will die. Such is the way of men."

"And will you also die then, when men forget about you?" he asked.

She laughed scornfully. "I was here when this world was born, and I shall be here when it dies, and when it becomes a cold cinder, I'll leave and travel through space to find another home, another green planet of earth and water and living things to live among," she said. "I am an immortal, a tiny part of the force that lies behind this universe. You have seen me as a young woman and an old one. Neither is nearer to the truth than the other!"

"I don't understand," he said.

"You cannot until you become as I am, an immortal, a spirit," she said, "But I will try. In my world – or worlds – fantasy becomes reality and reality is fantasy. Would you like to share it with me? There's room for another spirit. You shall be merman to my mermaid!" She laughed as she invited him, but watched carefully for his reaction, her head cocked to one side.

"God – or whatever means the good, knows I am tired of this world of men," he said bitterly, "But I cannot envisage spending eternity in this lake, sweet though your company seems!"

At this the maid laughed so merrily that there was a sound again as of silver bells chiming and echoing through the night.

"I don't live here!" she said, "I am a water spirit, not bound to earth like a captive! If you come with me I shall show you many places on this planet, and if you become jaded with that, then there are many other worlds in this universe, strange and beautiful, to visit. Come!"

She extended her hand, and the man sat for a while, looking at her. Then he looked back at the lights of the villages below and sighed. Eventually he stood and shook his head.

"There is nothing down there for you," the maid urged. "But I cannot take you unless you come willingly, chance what the old tales tell of me. Come, mortal, and become a spirit! Give up your life and live!"

"One moment," the young man said. He reached into a pocket in his jacket and brought out the medals they had given him for the killings he had done in their name, a jumble of ribbons and silver metal in the moonlight and threw them far out into the lake.

"I am ready," he said simply, and as his body sank to the velvet turf a small white spark rose up from him and moved out, dancing lightly, across the surface of the lake, to where a green spark waited for him. They merged, blinked once, and were carried away on a light breeze that blew over the water.

They found the body of the young man the next day, lying curled up in his final sleep by the side of the Black Mere, and one man, as he took him up with the others to carry back down to the churchyard in the village, commented how at peace he looked, with what seemed to be a smile upon his lips.